THE SOFTER SIDE OF TEXAS

SAI MARIE JOHNSON

Published by Blushing Books
An Imprint of
ABCD Graphics and Design, Inc.
A Virginia Corporation
977 Seminole Trail #233
Charlottesville, VA 22901

Johnson, Sai Marie
The Softer Side of Texas

EBook ISBN: 978-1-61258-221-4
Print ISBN: 978-1-63954-037-2
v1

Early Mornings

T hey say in Texas the sky is as free and open as the prairie lands surrounding it. In the country, where city boys and girls just don't understand what it is like to really get in touch with your inner self but sometimes the world looks at the people there as if they are uneducated, or worse, pompous fools who know nothing except their guns, horses, and a stiff drink. In many ways, that was very true but for Ivanka Jessup, Texas was home. A crude and sometimes hard place to live, but nonetheless, it was still home. The blonde beauty had hair like the golden rays of sun as it filtered across the open desert and her skin was just as brilliant. In fact, Ivy Jessup's nickname from her father ended up being Honey Sunshine because of how sweet and pretty the young lady had always been. Judging a book by its cover would be foolish in the case of Ivy, however, because beneath all that decadence was a tomboy with a bite like a diamond rattler's. That morning was no different from any other morning and Ivy rolled over in her bed to moan aloud when the sunlight hit her eyes.

"It's too damn early!" she groaned, pulling the sheet back

over her face. Working the night shift at Bud's usually had this effect, and Ivy felt as if she was dying when the cock began crowing in the distance. Still living at home with her parents, the young woman had chores to run on her daddy's farm, but working late nights was beginning to take its toll on her. More than that, Ivy was starting to feel like she hated being the object of the customers' attention. Especially one in particular named Antonio Rodriguez. He was a Mexican-American farmhand who seemed to think he had the right to try to touch her, and like clockwork at about six o'clock every night, he would stride into her bar and demand a Tecate. It would be the start of at least a dozen others, and by eight o'clock that night, he would be well past the limit. For some reason, Bud didn't ever throw him out, though, and his actions towards Ivy never seemed to bother him, either. Ivy finally pulled herself out of bed and drew her hands up to tiredly wipe her eyes.

"Damn, this is killing me. I really need to find a new job." Yawning, she stood up and waltzed across her room to grab a pair of faded blue jeans which she shimmied on in a matter of seconds. Next, came a faded plaid button down which she tied off at her waist, and slipping her feet into a pair of tan boots, she opened the door to head to the kitchen. In the hallway, everything seemed to echo and Ivy could hear her parents discussing the bills already.

"Now, Jesse, you know we can't afford that. It is enough just keeping the horses fed. Ivy gives me all her money from working down at the bar, but I don't like the way Antonio looks at her. I worry about what could happen." Ivy's mother Margie's voice brushed past her ears, and Ivanka decided to wait in the hall a minute to listen in on what they were saying.

"Margaret, we can't have her quitting her job when you just said we can barely afford to keep feeding the animals. I know you don't want me to start looking for farmhands because of how much it will cost but I need the help. You and

Ivy can't help me with all of this. I need some manpower around here. If Ivanka quits her job, we'll definitely be up the creek. What else do you want me to do?" Jesse's voice was stern and pleading at the same time.

"Well, Jesse, I think we should consider getting our daughter into a new job and stop sending her down to work that biker bar. She's too sweet and pretty to be working there, and if one of those grimy men does something to her, you're going to regret it. Go hire a farmhand or two, I guess. I don't know what else we can do from here."

Ivy could hear her mother give a long sigh of disappointment and it was then she decided to ease out of the hallway and walk into the kitchen. "Good morning. What's for breakfast?"

Jesse and Margaret immediately shut their mouths. It was obvious to Ivy, they were attempting to keep this conversation between themselves, and because of the respect she had for her parents, she opted not to push the subject.

Margaret smiled pleasantly at her daughter as she looked back at her from the stove. "Pancakes, sausage links, and eggs, darling. Do you have to work tonight?" she asked gently. Most of the time she hated asking her daughter about work and it was because of what she was doing for a living. Not that Ivanka didn't work her tail off at the bar, but Margaret was a religious woman, and she knew places like that weren't places for good girls to be working. Ivy had always been a looker, but she was also a great student and had never brought her mama any amount of undue pain. Jesse and Margaret only had two children because Margie had difficulties with pregnancy. Unfortunately, Ivy's old brother, Brenton, passed away about two years before, in Afghanistan. It had been a devastating experience for their entire family but Ivy took it the hardest. Ever since then, Ivanka seemed to think it was her responsibility to take care of her parents and help them out with the ranch.

With a sigh, she smiled at her mother and nodded. "Yes, and tomorrow night, too. The usual schedule, Mama."

Jesse peered up from over his newspaper and watched Margie place a plate in front of his daughter. "You making decent tips still?"

Ivy nodded her head but the truth was ever since she had started having trouble with Antonio, her tips had gone down quite a bit. It didn't help that he had started bringing in a few buddies to heckle at her almost nightly, and it was starting to get the point that she really hated going in to work. Tonight would be worse, and she knew it, but telling her parents that would only make them worry more so she chose to let them believe things were working out just fine.

"Things are just fine; don't worry, I can handle my own, I promise." Ivy began to toy with her eggs in contemplation of how she was going to handle the night, but for now, she wanted to enjoy her breakfast before going out to help her dad with the farm chores.

Jesse adjusted the paper and looked back down on it with a nod of approval. "That's my tough girl. See, Margie, she can handle her own just fine. You worry too much," he retorted.

Margaret turned back to the stove and fidgeted in place. Jesse may have thought she was just fine, but Margie knew better. A mother always did know when something wasn't quite right with their child and Ivy's quick response left her wondering why she wasn't honest with them. She turned around to settle down beside her husband and nodded in agreement. "Yes, I know she's a tough cookie, just like her pa." Margaret chuckled to herself. It was never something that went over easily when she called him pa, and Jesse immediately brought the paper down to peer over the edge with furrowed eyebrows.

"Now listen here, woman. I ain't nobody's pa, pawpaw, or anything else. I see how ya are, wanting to make me old and cankered 'fore I'm ready to be. Just you remember, Margaret Anne Jessup, you ain't too far from being put out to pasture, yourself." He roared with laughter as his wife frowned and shook her head. These were the moments Ivanka really felt joy and peace. How could she ever tell her parents men were harassing her at work when it was her paychecks that helped put food on their table? She smiled and shook her head as her own laughter emitted her lips.

"You two are something else, teasing like high school kids," Ivy said. She finished eating the last bite of her meal and took a quick drink of orange juice before pushing her plate forward.

Margaret sat down and began forking her eggs into her mouth. She always had a habit of almost shoveling her food down in a hurry. One time, Ivanka had asked her why she ate so fast, and Margaret replied with an answer that seemed to fit with her reasoning. "There are way too many things to do around here and eating leisurely is what the cows do. I have work waiting on me." Her soft voice held a tinge of exhaustion to it, but it was that sense of duty that led Ivy to work so diligently in an occupation she herself despised. Her mind refocused on her parents, and she pushed her chair back to stand.

"I suppose I have a lot to do today, and I reckon that I'll be coming in late tonight. Dad, don't you worry about feeding the horses today. I'll go down to grain and water them now, before I head down to town to pay my cell phone bill. Do you need me to pay anything on any bills while I'm down there?" she asked.

Her father lowered the paper and glanced at her mom for a minute.

"You know, Ivy, you just pay the family share plan this month, and we'll handle the utilities. I think that would be the best. You really ought to have some fun or enjoy one of these fall festivals," Margaret replied. She always hated asking Ivanka to pay too much for the house bills and really wanted to see her daughter find a decent man. The loss of Ivy's brother had been a terrible occurrence for the entire family, but what pained Margaret the most now was seeing Ivanka work so hard in a place where men harassed her for what seemed to be nothing at all. A lot could be said about the bar and none of it was good, but Ivanka had the personality, body, and brains to be a great tender. She raked in tons of tips because of her bubbly sense of humor, but seeing her daughter as she was now just didn't sit right with Margaret, at all.

"Are you sure about that, Mom? I don't need to go to any of these shindigs out here. I get plenty of party action down there at the bar. To tell you the truth, I would rather go horse-back riding or target practicing. That's beside the point, though. Really, Mama, I have plenty of money to help out this month. You never know if it will stay that way next month, though. I want to help. Please don't limit me from adding to the pot just because you think I need to have more fun than I'm already having," Ivy said.

Margaret shifted in her seat and gave a sigh. She knew Ivanka's heart was definitely in the right place but, being a mother, she couldn't help wondering if maybe her daughter deserved more of a life than the one she had been handed.

"Ivy, can you go down to the co-op and post a flyer for me?" her father asked.

Ivanka peered back at him and gave a nod. "What kind of flyer are you posting, Dad?" she asked.

"Well, I'm looking to hire at least one ranch hand. I don't think you can help me with all the work down here all the time. Your mom is right; you need to have a little bit of a social life. Maybe even go on a shopping visit to Houston or something. You spend entirely too much time down there serving those riffraff and no time doing anything productive for yourself. You can also pay the water bill while you are down in town, if you are stuck on helping with something else besides the phone bills," he said.

Ivanka gave a sigh. Arguing with her parents now never seemed to work in her favor for long. She couldn't let on that she had overheard their conversation earlier, but she also felt really helpless in the situation. It seemed doing the right thing only ever amounted to feeling stuck either way but her father's request for help on the water bill gave her something to work with.

"I'll think about the shopping trip, Dad, and I will pay the phone bills, along with the water bill. See y'all in a bit," she said, waltzing out the door without giving them another chance to argue. She crossed the yard quickly and, pausing in the middle of the grass, breathed in gently. The air was sweet and smelled of an early autumn. It was Ivy's favorite time of the year. When she was a little girl, watching the leaves turn golden, the orange, red, and bronze hues of every plant had been her favorite pastime. It was a warm day, even for being an early November morning, but the weather had been awkward those past few weeks. Ivy preferred the warmth to winter any day, though, and it brought her spirits up as she walked into the stables. The family had eight horses stalled up. Four that belonged to them and four that were being paid to be cared for by the family. Ivanka went to the grain sack and lifted it to dump into a wheelbarrow. She tossed a scoop on top of it and began pushing it down the line.

"Hey ya, Mack," she said, scooping some grain up and dumping into the first horse's feeding tray. The animal snorted and leant down to begin munching. Ivy smiled and proceeded to the next horse stall. The nametag read Duchess, and Ivy grinned at the tawny colored animal. The name was fitting, and she had been a blue-ribbon winner repeatedly. She pranced over to the feeding tray and lowered her head to be petted. Ivy stuck her hand through the window and gently stroked the creature. She had always wanted to own Duchess but never had enough money to pay for her. Lately, her owners had neglected to come see her but Ivanka felt a sense of camaraderie with her and she never complained about their negligence. Rather, she hoped they would never come to collect or would cease paying their stall rental so she could claim ownership by default of payment. So far, they had yet to miss a payment and, truth be told, her owners were some of the few who kept their farm going. They owned two of the four animals. Duchess and Duke were their names. Duke was ornery and callous, most days, but Duchess always had a sweet demeanor, regardless of who fed her.

"You're always such a lady, Duchess," Ivanka said. She moved down the line and fed the rest of the animals. Next, came the watering; then, she got them each two flakes of hay. After the feeding frenzy was over, Ivanka exited the barn and headed back towards the house. It was about eleven in the morning and she was hoping to get some sleep before the evening Happy Hour rolled around. Chores and responsibilities seemed to be the entirety of her life, but sleep was the one thing she never seemed to get much of. She walked back into the house and went straight for her keys.

2

It's Duty

"**B**e careful downtown, Ivy!" Margaret called to her as she pulled her key ring off the nail beside the front door.

Ivanka slammed the door and called over her shoulder without hesitation, "Don't worry too much, Mama. I'll be back soon!" She jogged across the yard and hopped in her Datsun pickup truck. It was a get around vehicle, but so far, it had done her right. She remembered her brother helping her get the thing into decent shape enough to drive. As she threw the vehicle into reverse, her mind drifted off to think of the last thing he had said to her.

"Ivanka, you really should go to college away from here. There ain't a damn thing left around here for a girl like you to do," he had advised. Back then, Ivanka had considered going to college to become a veterinarian, but four months later, her brother had died and the economy bottomed out at about the same time.

Ivy sighed as she drove down the long dirt driveway towards the main road. It seemed to her that she was never going to get out of here and her obligation to her family was more important than chasing any dreams, at this point. She shifted her radio to a country station and pulled out onto the road. All she could think of was wishing she could go back to the last day she had seen her brother and how if she could have foretold the future enough to make sure she said the right thing to him. Now, she would never have a chance, but taking care of the farm and her parents seemed to be the best honor she could ever give his memory. That was why Ivy never quit the bar and that was the reason Ivanka had long given up the idea of marriage, a family, or any other career. Her parents had nobody else to turn to, and Ivanka wasn't about to leave them high and dry in times like these.

The trip to town was about ten miles and it usually took her no more than fifteen minutes. Today, she drove slower than usual, though, and what was a routine trip turned into a long drive filled with nostalgia. Ivanka shook her head upon the realization that she was wasting time and getting nowhere. She pulled up to the red light on Main Street and glanced over at the utility board. The phone company was directly across the street and she sat waiting for the light to change, wondering whom to pay first. As usual, Ivy chose to pay what her parents needed most before she paid for what she wanted. The light turned green and she pulled up to the water board to park. As she walked towards the building, a familiar catcall was screamed at her from across the street.

"Oye, mamacita! Come, let me get some of that!" Marco called to her. Ivanka turned around and shot him the bird before entering the building.

"Damn creep," she muttered under her breath. "Doesn't seem like he gets no. I thought it was the same in both languages," she continued as she came to the counter.

"Good morning, Ivy," the clerk, Mrs. Browning, said. "Having a bit of trouble today?" she asked.

Ivy shook her head and pulled out her wallet. "No, Mrs.

Browning, just annoyed and tired. Forgive my attitude this morning; it's just been one of those kinds of days." She smiled.

"You here to pay your mama and daddy's water bill?" Mrs. Browning inquired.

Ivy gave a nod and waited for her to tell her how much the bill was. "Yes, ma'am. How much is the damage this month?" she asked.

Mrs. Browning immediately began typing information into the computer and announced the amount gently, "Seventy dollars even, this month, dear. Paying cash again?" she asked.

"Like always, Mrs. Browning." Ivy took out three twenties and a ten-dollar bill and handed it to her with a nod.

"I figured, hun." Mrs. Browning never said anything rude to Ivanka, but she got the feeling she didn't approve of her job any more than her mother did. It didn't help that Ivy had been a star student and a cheerleader at one time. Everyone figured the young woman was bound for great things like her brother, but when she ended up becoming a bartender at the biker bar, a lot of people had begun putting their noses down on her. Ivanka took it in stride and remained silent as Mrs. Browning keyed in the payment and printed off her receipt.

"It's just easier to use my tips and get things handled. Thanks for your help, Mrs. Browning," Ivy said, taking the receipt and exiting quickly. She jogged back across the street, making certain to see if Marco was still anywhere in the vicinity. When she noticed the coast was clear, she entered the phone store and strode up to the counter. The process went about the same as it had at the utility board, but Ivanka kept her mouth silent for the duration of her time there. They man who ran the phone company spoke little English, and it made her uncomfortable that she could hardly understand a word he said. Even in a small town like hers, it seemed that foreigners were everywhere. After she paid the bill, she crossed the street and got back into her car. Moments later, Ivanka was headed back down the same road towards her house and ready to hit the hay faster than a June bug against a windshield. She pulled back into the driveway and crept the Datsun to a stop.

As she entered the house, it didn't take long to notice her mother taking a catnap on the couch while soap operas played on the television. She shook her head and went to her room, taking care not to wake her mother as she eased herself into her bed. Work came at four o'clock that day, allowing her about three hours to sleep. As usual, Ivy stared at the ceiling and drifted into a light slumber.

3

Work Sucks, I Know

The sound of the alarm blaring brought Ivanka out of her slumber quickly. She sat up to glance at the clock and threw her palm down on the silent button with a slap. Annoyed by how quickly the time had passed, Ivy slipped out of bed and lazily opened her door. Both of her parents were sitting in the living room, watching CNN, as usual. Ivanka strode to the bathroom and turned on the shower, allowing the room to fill with steam. It was her usual routine. She slid into the shower and washed herself quickly. As soon as she stepped out of the water, she wiped her hand across the mirror and began the process of putting on her face. That was what her mother always called it. Getting herself dolled up just to go work her butt off for a bunch of drunken fools. Fools who paid a pretty tip to bartenders with pretty faces and sweet attitudes. Ivanka shimmied her apple bottom into a tight-fitting pair of jeans then put on her cowboy boots. A suede cowboy hat completed the look, and a sheen gloss across the lips left her with a mouth yearning for the right man's kiss. A man who seemed to exist only in her dreams and chick flicks.

Ivy smiled and exited the bathroom quickly. She waved to her mom and dad before grabbing her keys off the key ring again.

"I'll be in at the usual time, around one or so," she said before slamming the front door. The drive was a quick one, and soon, she found herself pulling into the bar parking lot with a grimace. "Damn it," she murmured as she noticed Antonio's Ford Ranger parked at the front. She eased herself out of the vehicle and crossed the lot to enter through the back. Bud wasn't about to keep Antonio off the lot because he was one of his biggest paying customers. Even if he had caused a scene a time or two, it seemed like he got away with it every chance he could, and Ivy had really gotten to where she loathed seeing the bastard. As she walked into the back, she heard Bud on the phone with a beer vendor.

"Now, I ordered that damn Tecate a week ago! It was supposed to be coming in tonight. How in the hell am I supposed to cater to my Hispanic customers without one of their favorite brews on the tap?" he squealed into the receiver. Ivy knew, at that moment, he was in one of his usual moods, and it made her frown even more. She decided not to say a word and just walked to the register, where she clocked in and began counting down her till, as she always did. Bud got off the phone and glanced over at her with a reddened face.

"Afternoon, Ivy. Hope you are ready to deal with a bunch of pissed off Mexicans. We ain't going to have no Tecate for another three days," he stated.

Ivy's eyebrows rose and she gave a slight nod, keeping her eyes focused on the cash at hand. "Well, that sounds like a whole lot of fun, boss," she said quietly.

Bud's eyes ran down her body and back to the till she was counting. "You think you can go down to the store and buy us a couple twelve packs to serve longnecks tonight?" he asked.

Ivy stopped counting the money and looked back at him. "I saw Antonio's already parked out front. You planning on keeping the bar closed long enough for me to get down there and pick it up? I really don't want to come in to a full bar of angry Mexicans who have a tendency of giving me a hard time, as it stands," she said matter-of-factly.

Bud groaned and shook his head. "That's money, Ivanka. How am I supposed to run a business if I keep my doors locked just so you can go pick us up some beer?" he asked. If there was one thing for certain about Bud Hawkes, he didn't like losing a profit for anything. A real stickler of a man, but someone who had been running a successful bar for thirty-five years, Bud didn't get a reputation like he had for nothing.

Ivanka pursed her lips and gave a nod. "Yeah, I figured as much," she said. It was a hard feat to keep her cool, but Ivanka was a resilient young woman, and she had no other options at this point. Ivy held out her hand and smiled. "Well, give me the money for the honey, boss man," she said sweetly.

Bud smiled and reached into his pocket to pull out a couple of fifty-dollar bills. "Tell John, I'm going to need all the imported beer he's got on stock right now. Shouldn't be too much, but that ought to cover it," he said.

Ivy nodded and turned around to lock up the register. "I'm starting with a hundred and fifty, tonight. Tell Sue to stay the hell off my register, Bud. Last time, I was twenty short and I am not about to lose that money again because of a ditzy redhead. I don't care how sweet her butt is or how much attention she brings the bar. I'm not going to be paying for her dumbassery again," Ivy stated, taking the money and exiting. The great thing about the store was that the people down there were always nice to her and, a few times, the owner, John, had offered her a job. The only problem was it didn't pay as much as Bud did and the hours were even less than the bar's. If her parents had more clients at the farm, Ivy would have loved to work for the Hughes family. At this point, there was no need to drive so she crossed the road quickly and headed into the grocer's. Molly Richards was standing behind the counter with a smile on her face, the moment her eyes fell on Ivanka. She was a petite brunette who was an under-classman in high school. It was her senior year, now, and Ivy had been her coach during cheerleading camp, a few years before.

"Ivanka!" Molly exclaimed, excited to see her tutor again.

"Hey, Molly. How are things going?" she asked with that famous smile of hers.

"Oh, I just started working here yesterday. I'm trying to save up some money to buy a new car before I graduate next spring. I plan on going up state to school, and Mr. Hughes offered to let me run the register for him, after school," she said.

Ivy gave a nod and placed her hands on the countertop. "Is John here today? I need to buy some beer for the bar, and I don't think they'll let you sell it to me," Ivanka stated.

Molly gave a nod and walked into the back. A few moments later, John exited the office and frowned.

"Bud sent you over to get some beer again, Ivy? What the hell is going on over there, having to send somebody to buy up all the grocery store beer? Doesn't he keep his bar stocked at all?" John said.

Ivy started laughing and leaned into the counter. "The vendor is behind schedule, I guess, and he is plum out of the Mexican imports. You know we get a lot of rowdy Hispanics in there, and if we don't have the right poison, they can be a real handful, let me tell you," Ivanka said.

"So what's he want you to pick up today, Ivy?" John asked.

"Tecate and Corona. He said he wants all the stock you will let him purchase," she replied.

John gave a snort and motioned for Ivanka to follow him to the back. "Come on back, Ivy. Let's see what I can get for you. Molly, watch the front for me, hun," John murmured.

Ivanka crossed behind the counter and followed John towards the stockroom.

As they approached the beer cooler, John turned around and grimaced. "You know I wish you didn't work for that asshole," he said bluntly.

"Yeah, me, too, but I need my job, John. There aren't any other places in town that pay or offer as many hours as Bud does, unfortunately. Trust me, Mom and Dad have been harping at me a lot, lately, about it. I think Mom really wants me to quit, but I just can't do that," Ivy stated.

John Hughes had been a childhood friend of Ivy's father and his son, Matthew, had gone into the military with her brother. They had gone in, intending to be battle buddies, but Matthew came back whole. Ivanka's brother came back in a body bag. Ivy sighed and pulled out the money Bud had given her.

"How much do you think you can spare for two hundred dollars?" Ivanka asked.

John looked over the cases of beer and pursed his lips as he thought. "I guess we could go with five or six cases. That should at least hold you off for the night. I hope," he said.

"All right, do you think you can help me carry them across the street?" she asked.

John gave a nod. "Yeah, with Molly here to run the front, I can handle helping bring them over there. Let's get them paid for and get the receipt and I'll haul them over there in the golf cart," John said.

Ivy nodded and followed him back to the counter, where he entered the amount and checked her out. Ivy took the receipt and placed it, with the change, back in her pocket as John went to the back and began loading up the beer. Ivanka watched in silence as he readied it all and pointed at the passenger seat.

"Ready to go, John?" Ivanka asked as she sat down. He

nodded and rolled across the road to the back of the bar. John pulled into the parking lot, and Ivy hopped off the back to open the backdoor. Immediately, John began unloading the beer, and Ivy walked inside to give Bud the receipt and let him know John was at the back, unloading.

"Bud!" Ivanka called as she walked towards the office.

"Yeah, Ivy?" he said, exiting the room.

"John's in the back with the beer. Here's the receipt and change." She held it out to him and waited for him to take it. Bud gave a nod and took the items. Ivanka turned to walk towards the front of the bar, leaving the two men to handle the inventory.

"Got work to do!" she called over her shoulder. As Ivy walked out behind the counter, she noticed that Antonio and a friend of his named Luis were sitting in their usual corner. A roll of the eyes brought Ivy to turn around as her coworker sauntered over.

"Hey ya, Ivy," Sue announced.

Ivanka gave a wave and began wiping down her counter. "Hi, Sue," she said nonchalantly. Sue McGee was a woman with a reputation, and it wasn't a good one. Rumor had it that, years before, she had worked in Las Vegas as a stripper. Ivy had been nice to her at first, but recently, her drawer kept coming up short. The only person who seemed to be a culprit was Sue, but Ivy had never been able to prove it. So, there she stood, attempting to be nice to her co-worker. A co-worker who just didn't seem to get the point that Ivanka couldn't stand being around her, let alone having a conversation with her. Just then, Antonio pushed his chair back and walked over to the bar.

"Oye, Ibanka," he said.

Ivy shuddered and grit her teeth before turning around. "Hello, Antonio. You need something?" she asked.

"Yeah, I need some of that sweet cola," he said with a smirk.

Cola didn't mean Coca-Cola. It meant he wanted some of Ivy's backside, and she wasn't about to be disrespected in any language. "Antonio, the only cola we serve here is Coca-Cola. Unless you want a rum and Coke, I think you ought to go sit back down," Ivy stated flatly.

Antonio's chuckles continued. "No, you always tell me no. I get sick of dat," Antonio replied. "Ju know I come here ebery day to see you, Ibanka." He always had a habit of using a b where the v was supposed to be.

"Yeah, you've been telling me that every day since you came here," Ivanka replied.

"Ju don't like me, eh?" Antonio asked.

"You just now getting the idea, Antonio?" Ivy responded.

Antonio's face fell into a frown and he reached over the bar to pull Ivanka's arm.

Sue's face went white. "Bud! Get up here!" Sue called, but by the time she was able to say a word, Ivanka had already reacted. She grabbed the draft hose and squirted Antonio right between the eyes.

"Sorry, Antonio, I think you need a hose-down!" Ivanka said, continuing to shoot him with the draft beer.

"Ey! Ju bitch!" Antonio screamed.

Behind him, his buddy, Luis, was roaring with laughter. "Mire ese vato!" he said, which meant look at this guy.

"Yeah, I'm a bitch, but you're a dickhead!" Ivanka insulted him just as Bud walked out of the back.

"Hey! Damn it, what the hell is going on here?" Bud screamed as he took a look around the bar.

"I was just giving Antonio a hose-down, Bud. Seems the man doesn't understand what no means and he got a little touchy-feely," Ivanka said.

Bud's face didn't give hint to him understanding what she was meaning, but the words he said next made it clear he didn't give a rat's ass about his employees or their personal space. "Damn it, Ivanka! You just wasted draft beer and insulted one of our best customers? You're fired!" he screamed.

Ivanka's face immediately fell into a shocked expression. "What the hell do you mean I'm fired? This asshole just grabbed me, after asking for some of my ass! Do you not give a fuck about your employees?" she asked accusingly.

Bud scoffed at her and pointed towards the front door. "Get your shit and get the hell out of my bar, Ivanka Jessup. You're fired!" he roared.

Ivy shook her head and put her hand on her hip. "All right, that's cool, Bud. When can I get my last fucking check?" she asked angrily.

Bud looked down at his watch and curled his lower lip into his mouth. "Tomorrow at noon, I'll have your last check, Ivy. You can pick it up then," he said matter-of-factly.

Ivanka glared past him at Antonio and strode straight back out the bar. She jogged over to her Datsun and eased into the vehicle. After a few minutes of sitting there, she realized the truck wasn't about to start and leaned her head into the steering wheel.

"Fuck!" she groaned, stepping out of the truck. By this time, it was already starting to get dark, but she knew if she didn't get ahead on walking, she wasn't about to get home for a long while. She pulled out her backpack and slammed the door of the truck, stomping off across the lot towards the road. Curses and murmurs slid past her lips, but she knew all she could do was keep walking. By the time she got onto the road, she was shaking her head in frustration, and hot tears had begun rolling down her cheeks. "Just what I fucking needed, to lose my job because of an asshole who can't understand what the fucking word no means!" she said aloud. She slipped her hand back down to her pocket and pulled out her cell phone, pressing the number one to speed dial her parents. The phone fizzled out and died the moment she pressed the button. It seemed tonight was just not going to be Ivy's night. Fuming, she continued her angry stride down the empty Texas road.

Ivanka had been walking for what seemed like an eternity, but in reality, it had only been about an hour. The road had been completely empty, and as far as the eye could see, there was nothing but desert. Empty drying cornfields and nothing else to accompany her. She had decided to keep walking down the road, hoping she would find a gas station or some-thing where she could contact her parents to explain the situation. It was just unbelievable that Bud had fired her over Antonio's grossly intimidating behavior. What astounded Ivy the most was that Bud didn't really seem to care that this man had grabbed her over the bar and that she had a right to defend both herself and his interests. Apparently, his human resources didn't much matter, and Ivy was still so shocked that she couldn't see how she would ever be nice to him when she went for her check the next day. Suddenly, the flicker of headlights rolled over the hill, and Ivy stood to the side of the road, watching, as a black Camaro pulled up beside her.

"Great," she muttered as a man rolled down his window and peered over at her.

"What are you doing walking this road out by yourself, miss?" he asked with a perked eyebrow.

Naturally, Ivanka assumed the worst and crossed her arms over her chest with a look of distrust. "Having a walk. What is it to you?" she asked.

The man immediately began to laugh slightly. "I'm sorry. Let me see if I can get this right this time," he said gently. "My name is Aaron Kilpatrick. I am trying to find a place called

Jessup Farm. I heard there might be a business opportunity there," he said with a kind voice.

"Jessup Farm?" Ivanka's eyebrow lifted in uncertainty but she had remembered her father talking about taking an ad out, recently. "That's my father's farm," she said.

"Oh, well, is it somewhere close by, then?" Aaron asked.

"It's another thirty-minute walk, at least," she muttered.

"Um, so you are walking that far? Mind if I ask why?" Aaron inquired.

Ivy gave a huff and lowered her head. "I got fired from my job and my pickup wouldn't start so I kind of had to start walking," she replied.

Aaron's eyes widened and he looked back in his vehicle for a moment. After a few seconds, he held out a cell phone. "Do you need to make a call?" Aaron offered the phone as he asked.

Ivanka found the man was actually being very generous, but her first instinct was not to trust him in the least. "Um, yeah, sure, thanks." Ivy held out her hand and took the phone. Immediately, she began dialing the number for her parents but nobody answered.

"No answer, I take it?" Aaron asked when Ivy handed the phone back.

"No, doesn't look like it. Shit," she said aloud.

Aaron chuckled. "I can offer you a ride, since we are going to the same place, if you want," he offered.

As Ivy looked at the man, she noticed he was surprisingly very attractive and about the same age as she was. He had sandy blond hair and vibrant green eyes, with an olive complexion that screamed tanner or someone who spent a lot of time in the sun. What shocked Ivanka was the fact he was driving a speed demon car instead of a truck or get around vehicle. She wondered if he had money, and if so, what had brought him out here?

"Um, I guess I really don't have many other options right now. Mind if I ask you what you're doing looking for my dad's farm, anyway?" she inquired. It suddenly occurred to her that it probably looked really awkward for her to be standing there with this stranger on the side of the road. She walked around to the passenger's side and eased herself into the car.

Aaron smiled and began explaining his story. "Well, I'm here for a job as a ranch-hand. I've got a lot of experience working horses and I've driven a few tractors. I saw your dad's ad in the paper and wanted to see about coming down for a job. It's a three-hour drive from where I'm from and I figured I would get a motel, once I got here, so I could go see him in the morning," he said.

Ivanka wondered whether or not her dad would like this guy, but it seemed he had some manners, and Ivanka knew that was one thing her dad would approve of. Her mother would delight in his country charm, and Ivy was beginning to think he was a savior at a moment she needed one most. She smiled pleasantly and adjusted her seatbelt.

"Oh, let me guess, you got ahold of one of my dad's flyers or ads? He's been looking for somebody to help, for a while. You know the job comes with room and board, right?" Ivy asked.

"Yeah, I read that. I didn't know giving the boss man's daughter a ride in the middle of the night was a part of the job description, though. Not that I'm upset about it, at all," he said.

The vehicle was in good condition, and the driver was really starting to win her over with his enchanting demeanor. Ivy felt like Cinderella swooning over a prince, and she had just met the guy.

"Yeah, well, it's about ten miles down the road here. You'll take a left on to Decaturville Drive, and the farm's about a mile down the road there, on the right," she directed.

Aaron nodded and threw the car into drive again but he eased up to speed, which surprised her.

"Wow, safe driver there, Aaron?" Ivy asked.

"Yeah, well, as fast as this baby can go, I can't afford the parts it takes to put her back together if I ride her too hard," he said with a slight chuckle.

"You've got some sense of humor there, cowboy," she said in response. She was already rooting for him in the back of her mind. Ivy could see this guy working the land and helping her dad at the ready. He had the kind of personality that spoke gratitude and good raising. Just the kind of guy she figured no longer existed.

"Well, so tell me something about your farm, then, and I didn't catch your name," he said.

Ivy fidgeted in realization that she hadn't even told him who she was yet. "Oh, Ivy, or Ivanka, Jessup. Whichever you want to use," she said.

"Ivanka? Isn't that Russian? Where did your parents come up with that?" he asked.

"My mother's best friend in high school was a foreign exchange student. It was her name. Mom fell in love with it and I was the namesake, I guess," Ivanka replied.

"Well, it's a beautiful name, Ivy," Aaron said.

The rest of the drive went by quickly, and Ivy found herself staring out the window in silence. It didn't take long for them to pull into the driveway. Ivanka could see the lights on in the house, and as Aaron parked, she opened the door gently. "Stay here and let me go get my parents. The dogs may be out, and I would hate for you to get bitten in five seconds of being here," she announced. She didn't wait for Aaron to give a reply, jogging across the yard and into the house quickly.

"Mom! Dad!" Ivanka called for her parents as she shut the door.

Margaret exited the living room and met Ivanka in the foyer. "What are you doing here, Ivy? Thought you weren't getting off work till one or so," her mom said.

"Yeah, well, I got some bad news about that, but first, there is a guy here who is interested in the ranch hand job. His name's Aaron Kilpatrick," Ivy explained.

Margaret perked a brow and peered out the window. "Driving a Camaro, and he wants to work a ranch?" Margaret asked.

"Mom, this guy is actually really nice. I was pleasantly surprised. Where's Dad?" Ivy asked.

"He's in the living room, asleep, but I'll go wake him up. Ask Camaro boy into the kitchen, and we'll meet you there," Margaret said.

Ivy nodded and went back out the door.

"Honey, wake up," Margaret said, shaking her husband back from slumber.

He shifted and cracked an eye to look at her. "What's the deal, Margaret? I'm trying to get my some shut-eye here," he said.

"Ivanka just came home with some young man named Aaron Kilpatrick. Says he is here about the ranching job, and I don't know why Ivy's with him, but her truck ain't outside," Margaret explained.

Jesse sat up and looked back at her, perplexed. "Where's the kid?" he asked.

"They're coming to meet us in the kitchen, now."

Like clockwork, the moment Margaret said that, Ivy entered the house with Aaron in tow. Jesse stood up and brushed past his wife as he went towards the kitchen. He walked in to see his daughter and the stranger seated directly across from one another at the kitchen table.

Aaron stood up and extended his hand. "Good evening, sir. I'm sorry about coming so late, but I drove three hours to discuss this job offer. I've already met your daughter, and I just wanted to say thank you for agreeing to talk to me now," he said.

Jesse sized the boy up in a glance and shook his hand. "What's your name, kid?" he asked.

"Aaron Kilpatrick," Aaron replied.

"All right, Aaron. What have you done for work in the past?" Jesse asked as he glanced over at Ivanka.

"Well, sir, I've been working with horses all my life. I was raised on a ranch outside of Houston, and I know how to drive a tractor. I've harvested hay, corn, and soybeans. Just about everything you can think of, at some point or another. For the past year, I worked at a car mechanic shop but they went under, due to the economy. I've been looking for a good job ever since, but they're not so easy to come by right now," Aaron explained.

"Yeah, I know what you mean, kid. Well, I can't pay a heck of a lot. This is base pay with room and board. There's an apartment above the barn, and that was where I was planning on letting the help live while working here. I'll handle the utilities up there and all that mess, but you've got to pay for your own food or cable, if you want it. Pay's nine dollars an hour, and it works out to be about forty hours a week. Chores are really easy, right now, but harvesting is about to come about here, shortly. Does that sound like a decent offer?" Jesse asked.

Aaron drew his right hand up and trailed a finger under his chin. "Yeah, sounds good to me. I think this will work out real nicely," he said, holding his hand out to shake Jesse's again.

"Well, since you're already here, I guess we can show you to the apartment, right?" Jesse said, shaking his hand again.

Ivanka smiled as she watched the exchange between the two men. She was feeling really ecstatic, and Margaret gave a knowing glance at her.

"Sure thing, Mr. Jessup. I'll follow your lead," Aaron said. Jesse exited with Aaron following. They left the two women to gawk.

"So, are you going to tell me how you got caught up with that nice-looking boy tonight, Ivy?" Margaret asked, eyeing her daughter.

"Well, it was really by accident, Mama. Bud fired me tonight for shooting Antonio down with draft beer after he tried to grab me," Ivy said.

"What? That jerk fired you for not wanting a scumbag grabbing you?" Margaret's eyes widened, and her face began to grow red. It was obvious to any bystander that she wasn't too happy about what she had just heard.

"Yeah, he fired me. Then, my Datsun wouldn't start, and I had to walk," Ivy said.

"Why didn't you call me to pick you up?" her mom asked.

"'Cause the phone died and I couldn't. So, I started walking down the road, and here shows up this guy, asking for directions to the farm," Ivy said.

"You hopped in a car with a stranger who asked for directions? That wasn't too smart, Ivanka," her mother reprimanded.

"I didn't just hop in his car, Mom. He let me use his cell, and you didn't answer. I gave him the short interview before I ever got into the car. I'm smarter than you think," Ivanka said.

"Well, I guess you got here safe, and that is what is most important," Margaret stated.

"Yeah, and it looks like you got someone to help with the farm now. So, it all paid off, right?" Ivy asked.

"I don't know, seems to me you've got a fancy for this kid. Can't say I blame you; he's a looker, for sure." Margaret chuckled.

"Mom, I just met him. Let's be realistic here. I don't think he's about to marry me at the sunrise, ya know," Ivanka said.

"Well, that may be true, but the way you were looking at him, I'd say you were rooting for him, long before he ever got that interview with your dad," Margaret replied.

"Maybe so, Mom, but you did tell me you wanted me to start looking around and doing something different. Guess I'm out of a job, and there's a welcome distraction working the farm. I blame you. You spoke this into being, and now it is," Ivy said with a wink.

Margaret chuckled and nodded. "Seems you may be right, Ivy. I just hope this Aaron Kilpatrick turns out to be what we need around here. Been a while since we had anyone else on the land. It's going to be an interesting transition.

Ivanka gave a nod of agreement and leaned back in her chair.

"Yeah, I think you are right, Mama."

4

New Beginnings

The following morning, Ivanka awoke to the sound of the cock crowing and men talking outside of her bedroom window. She peeked outside and noticed her dad already loading hay bales onto the back of his pickup truck with Aaron's help. She smiled as she watched the two of them and listened to their morning conversation.

"So, you like football, Aaron?" Jesse asked.

Aaron gave a nod. "Yeah, but I'm personally an Alabama fan. I know that don't hold too well in Texas." He chuckled.

Jesse laughed and nodded. "Well, I got to give it to them elephants; they're a hell of a team, for sure. That many national championships under your belt, you would have to be. I'm a Texas fan, myself, but I'll watch an Alabama game. If you want to see a football game, they're the team to keep your eyes on," Jesse agreed.

"I always thought so. I played running back in high school and hoped someday I might be able to play college. Didn't happen, though, but ya know, that's life, right?" Aaron said.

"I know what you mean, kid. I wanted the same thing, but Margaret wound up pregnant with our oldest kid, our last year of high school. I felt like I had to do the right thing by her and at least make her an honest woman. That's the way it works. Life always throwing in a wrench where we least expect it," Jesse said.

"Was that Ivy?" Aaron asked.

"No, that was my son, Brenton. He joined the Army, about a year ago, but he didn't make it back," Jesse said, leaning against the truck.

Aaron looked down and sighed. "My best friend didn't, either. He was like the brother I never had. It's been about two years now. Sorry to hear about your son. Nothing worse than losing a loved one," Aaron stated solemnly.

"Yeah, it's been real hard on the girls. Hell, I would be lying if I didn't say it wasn't hard on me, too. I'm proud of my boy's legacy, though. He did what he thought was right, and that's all a father can ask for," Jesse said.

"I can see where you would be real proud. I'd have joined the Army, myself, but things ended up working out where I had to take care of my granddad. He got real sick. Actually, he just passed, about three months ago," Aaron said.

Ivanka slipped away from the window. She went into the kitchen to sit down and yawned.

"Morning, Ivy," Margaret said as she brought a cup of coffee to the table.

Ivy smiled and reached for the mug. "Thanks, Mama. I see that Dad and Aaron are already working hard," she said.

"Yes, it would seem they are. They had breakfast and went on their way. Aaron's a real nice boy. I think your dad's taking a liking to him real fast," Margaret replied.

Ivy brought the mug to her lips and blew over the liquid. "Yeah? Well, I'm real hungry. What's for breakfast?" she inquired.

Margaret gave a smile and placed a platter of steaming

eggs, bacon, and pancakes in front of her daughter. "Country breakfast, as usual, hun," Margaret said.

"Wow, Mom, you outdid yourself today," Ivy said, lifting a fork to begin cutting into the pancakes. "Sure looks good," she finished.

Margaret sat down beside her and folded her hands as she watched Ivanka eat. "So, what are you planning on doing about work now, Ivy?" she asked curiously.

"Well, I've got to get the truck from Bud's, somehow. I figured I'd do that when I went to get my check. You think Dad can tow it back for me?" Ivy asked.

Margaret nodded and pursed her lips. "Yeah, we can get the winch out and bring it in. Didn't Aaron say he used to work as a mechanic?" Margaret asked.

Ivanka looked back at her mother as if she was following her train of thought. "Yeah, I think he did say that. Why, what you thinking, Mama?" Ivy asked.

"Well, maybe he could fix the Datsun for you? You could ask him," Margaret said.

Ivanka shoveled some eggs into her mouth and chased them away with a gulp of coffee. "Well, I guess I could, but I don't know, Mom," Ivy said nervously. There was something about Aaron Kilpatrick that had really started to settle into Ivanka's bones. She had just met the guy but, already, she knew she was going to have a hard time not growing attached to him with his presence being an everyday occurrence. All she could think was that she didn't want to put too much burden on him.

"What don't you know, Ivy? Ask him, or else all your last check is going to go on getting that old beater fixed up, and you're not going to have any money to look for a new job with," Margaret stated matter-of-factly.

Ivanka frowned and looked up at her mother with a shake of the head. "Why do you always have to best me with all that wisdom of yours, Mama? I don't want to burden the boy down with tons of work when Daddy needs his help around here. I guess I will ask him, though," she said.

Margaret grinned and stood up to look out the window. "When do you want to go downtown for your truck and check, then?" she asked.

Ivanka finished eating her breakfast and pushed the plate forward. "I guess whenever you are ready. I need to go get dressed, first, and tell Dad to get the truck," she said.

"Don't worry about it, Ivy. I'll go tell your dad to get the truck ready. You go get a shower and get yourself dressed," Margaret said.

Ivanka gave a nod and walked out of the kitchen while Margaret walked out the door. Margaret crossed the yard and called out to her husband from a distance, "Jesse! We need the truck to haul the Datsun back from town!"

Jesse turned around and looked at his wife before passing a glance back at Aaron. "Well, I guess that means it's time to get a move on, Aaron. Ready to help me get Ivy's beater from town and manage not to beat her old boss, at the same time?" he asked. There was one thing about Jesse Jessup and that was that he didn't like Bud from the get-go. He had tolerated and supported his daughter having a job because the family needed the extra income, but Bud had it coming to him, and Jesse was going to have a difficult time not punching his lights out, once he got there.

Aaron's eyebrows lifted, and he chuckled. "Well, you think this guy needs his butt whooped, maybe we ought to give it to him." Aaron stated.

Jesse laughed and nodded. "I would say yeah, but I ain't got the money to bail your butt out of jail, right now. Though I got some choice words to say to that bastard, once I see him. Do you know the story of what went on down there? There's this Hispanic kid who keeps harassing Ivy, and he tried to grab her. I just don't see how that asshole could fire my daughter for defending herself from a piece of shit like that," Jesse muttered. It wasn't normal for him to use cuss words, but at that point, he had just about had his fill of Antonio's antics and Bud not doing a thing to defend his daughter at work. Now that Ivanka was unemployed, Jesse didn't worry too much about what could happen down at the bar, but he did worry about what Antonio may try next. He was beginning to wonder if the guy wasn't above rape, and if he had already tried to grab Ivanka, what would he do next?

5

Choices

I vanka, Jesse, and Aaron all sat in the truck, riding down
the road to old Bud's bar. Ivy sat comfortably in the
middle of them, but the proximity to Aaron was something she was having a hard time with. The night before had
made it difficult to notice how handsome the man honestly
was, but now, sitting just inches from him, Ivanka got to see
exactly what kind of physique Aaron had. He was well
sculpted, and if she had to make a guess at how tall he was,
she would have assumed he was about five-foot-ten with a
weight of a hundred and seventy pounds of pure muscle. She
could tell he had to work out or played sports most of his life.
Then again, Ivanka knew that farm work had a way of
keeping a person in their best shape possible. Aaron had
scooted as far towards the door as he could, and Ivanka knew
it was to give her some personal space. Even that aspect about
him was a pleasant surprise.

"So, Aaron, tell me about your family," Ivanka said in an
attempt to start up a conversation.

Aaron looked back at her and shrugged. "Well, there ain't
a whole lot to say, Ivy. My parents died when I was six, and

my grandparents raised me from then. Grandma passed away when I was fifteen, and it was just me and my granddad, up until about three months ago," he explained.

Ivy's face flat lined and she frowned. "I'm sorry to hear that. What about a girlfriend?" she asked curiously.

Jesse glanced over at her and gave a half grin. "Why you worried about his girlfriend, Ivy? Let the man have some privacy," Jesse stated.

Aaron chuckled and shook his head. "Nah, there ain't nothing to keep private there, Mr. Jessup. I don't have a girlfriend, Ivanka. I haven't really had the time for a girlfriend in the past year because my granddad was sick and I was taking care of him, in between working to support us both. Unfortunately, my granddad didn't leave me much but that car of mine," Aaron said.

Ivy started to feel like she could relate to Aaron and smiled.

"Yeah, that is about the same way it is with my Datsun. My brother got it running for me before he went into the military," Ivy stated.

The three of them pulled into the parking lot of the bar just then and Ivy sighed unpleasantly.

"You're not looking forward to this, are you, Ivy?" Aaron asked.

Ivanka shook her head and waited for her dad to step out of the vehicle. "Not one bit, Aaron. I've got a lot of vinegar in me after what Bud allowed to happen last night, but I guess I've got to make nice for the time being, right?" she said.

Aaron slid out of the truck and offered his hand to help Ivy outside. "Do you want me to go in with you and make sure everything goes alright?" he asked with a concerned expression.

Ivanka smiled and gave a nod as she slid her hand into his. "Yeah, that would be real nice of you, Aaron. Dad, can you get the truck started without any help or give us long enough to go in and deal with jerkoff, inside?" Ivanka said.

Jesse nodded and waved them off. "You two just hurry and get back out here so we can get on our way. I don't want to have to go in there to whip Bud's ass today," Jesse stated, walking towards the front of the truck, where he began pulling the winch out.

Aaron smiled and waved Ivanka before him, following in her footsteps towards the bar. As he walked behind her, Ivanka found herself smiling at the fact she had such a good-looking escort to waltz in after her. It was a feeling she had never experienced, and for the first time, she was beginning to think having a protective male's influence in her life may be a good thing. The two of them walked into the bar to find Bud sitting on a stool.

"Well, good morning to you, Ivanka," Bud said. "You ready to apologize and come back to work tonight? I thought a day off may cool you down some," he stated with a cocky grin.

Ivanka's face reddened in an instant, and she held out her hand.

"I'm ready to get my check and get out of here, Bud. You got it ready?" she asked.

Bud frowned and lifted an envelope from the counter. "Ya know, you could be sweet sometimes and get a heck of a lot further in life, Ivanka Jessup," Bud said.

Ivy took the envelope and tore it open, reading over the check amount. "I don't really care about being sweet to people who don't look out for their employees' interests. You know things like that get you loyal workers, but in your case, you wouldn't know a good employee from your ass, any day of the week."

Behind her, Aaron stifled a chuckle and crossed his arms.

"What the hell are you laughing at?" Bud peered at him past Ivanka.

"Whatever I damn well please, and what difference does that make to you? Ivy, you ready to go?" Aaron said.

Bud looked over Aaron, as if he was sizing him up, and stood up from the stool.

"Who the hell is this kid, Ivy?" he asked, nodding towards Aaron.

"None of your business, Bud, and by the way, fuck you." She smiled with a wink and strode past Aaron to exit the bar. Bud's mouth dropped as Aaron gave a nod and followed behind her.

"Like the lady said," he murmured, exiting the bar.

Bud stared at the two with his mouth agape in shock. If his expression was any indicator, he hadn't expected Ivanka Jessup to turn him down.

Ivy and Aaron strode over to Jesse, who had already began pulling the Datsun up onto the tow.

"How did things go?" Jesse asked, when noting the two coming towards him.

Aaron chuckled and waved towards Ivy. "Your daughter here knows how to handle herself, I'd say," Aaron stated.

Jesse gave a knowing nod and smiled at Ivanka. "Yeah, she got that from her mom. I take it you gave Bud a run for his money?" Jesse asked.

Ivanka laughed. "I don't think old Bud expected it, but I let him know where he could go, for sure," Ivy said.

"How much did he give ya on that last check?" Jesse inquired.

Ivy looked up at him and sighed. "He gave me what he owed me, but it isn't anything like the usual. He actually asked me to come back to work tonight. Said he was giving me the night off last night to cool me down. I think he honestly must've thought I'd be begging for my job back," Ivy said.

Jesse waved at the two as he walked back to the vehicle. "Well, let's get out of here before the bastard comes out asking for another chance he don't deserve," Jesse said, opening the door and pulling himself into the truck.

Aaron walked towards the door and opened it.

"After you, Miss Jessup." He ushered her towards the seat.

Ivanka smiled, slid her body back in the middle and crossed her legs. "You know something, Dad, I think I like this new employee of yours," Ivy said with a smile.

"Yeah, I think he will be a fine addition to the farm, myself." Jesse nodded, pulling out onto the road. As they continued down the road, a Ford Ranger pulled out in front of them, cutting them off at the light. Jesse fumed and leaned out the window.

"Hey, watch what the hell you're doing!" he yelled at the offender. Suddenly, the truck stopped in the middle of the road, and the driver flung the door open. There, standing before them, was Antonio, with a sneer on his face.

"Hey, you got a fucking problem, man?" he yelled across the road.

Jesse turned to glance over at Ivanka, whose mouth had fallen open.

"Oh, shit," Ivanka said.

Aaron opened the door and stepped outside, walking towards Antonio with a confused look.

"Something wrong, man? Did you not see us or something?" Aaron asked.

Antonio looked him over and bit his lip.

"No, I didn't. Maybe you and your friends should watch the fucking road, eh? You might get somebody killed out here," Antonio said.

Aaron furrowed his brow and crossed his arms, taking a loose stance. "Listen, I don't know what the problem is, but I don't really like your attitude. I didn't get out of the truck for any problems, but I am damn sure not going to be talked to like I did something wrong here, when you almost plowed into our front end," Aaron stated.

By this point, Jesse had stepped out of the truck, and Ivy was left staring at the scene in shock.

"Everything all right, Aaron?" Jesse asked as he approached the two men.

Antonio cast a glance back at the truck and took notice of the girl inside.

"Oh, you two got the bitch bartender with you, eh? I figured she was easy to get. Guess she has a problem with us tan people, eh?" he accused.

Aaron looked back at the truck and frowned. "You know, it's really not nice to talk about a lady like that. Didn't your parents teach you any manners or maybe you need somebody to teach your ass some," Aaron stated.

Ivanka slid out of the truck with her cell in her hand and walked towards the three men.

Jesse's fist clenched at his side, and he stared angrily back at the man.

"Hey, guys, let's just calm this down some, okay?" Ivy said as she approached.

Antonio glanced back at her and shook his head. "Nah, I think I got some things to say to you, puta," he said, but before he was able to say anything else, Aaron pulled his right hand back and slammed his fist into his chin.

"Don't call her that!" Aaron screamed as Antonio fell back in shock.

Jesse's eyes widened, and he stepped between the two. "Hey! That's about enough of that," Jesse said.

Ivanka stared at the two men, stunned, but Antonio wasn't about to listen to the old man's advice and flew at Aaron with both hands extended.

"I'm going to beat your fucking ass, mother fucker!"

Antonio bellowed as his hands came to clutch the collar of Aaron's shirt.

Aaron slid down and punched Antonio smack in the ribcage three times before pushing the man back against the pavement. In shock, Jesse pulled Aaron back before he was able to start kicking Antonio on the ground.

"Ivy, call the cops!" Jesse yelled as he pulled Aaron away from Antonio.

"You fucking asshole! I'm going to beat both your asses. Call the pinche policia, me vale verga!" Antonio screamed in anger.

Ivy shook her head and immediately began dialing the police department. It was just unbelievable to her that he had actually done all this, and she was beginning to wonder if her family had made a mortal enemy in Antonio. The dispatch officer answered, in a matter of seconds.

"Yes, hello, I need to report a traffic incident that has resulted in domestic assault," Ivanka said. The woman took the information and Ivy closed the flip quickly.

Jesse pulled Aaron back towards the truck and shook his head as Antonio stood there with a look of pure hatred on his face.

"If I were you, Antonio, I'd stay my ass right there and wait on the police. I've about had it with your shit," Jesse said.

Ivy shook her head and leaned against the truck, waiting for the police to show up. It took them about five minutes, considering the station was just around the corner from the incident.

Officer Kelvin Matthews slammed his patrol car door and strode over to them first. "Mind telling me what happened here, Jesse?" he asked.

Jesse gave a sigh and pulled Kelvin over to the shoulder. "Listen, Kelvin, the new kid is my new ranch hand, and Antonio began this mess. I don't want to see my employee get arrested, but I've got to be honest. Antonio pulled out in front of me and almost plowed into my truck. Aaron got out to try to calm Antonio down when he got angry about the situation. Needless to say, Antonio instigated a fight and Aaron knocked him for a loop," Jesse explained.

Kelvin pursed his lips and nodded. "All right, let me get his statement, and I'll be right back to get the rest," Kelvin stated, turning to walk towards Antonio, who sat on the curb near his vehicle.

"Hey, Antonio, what happened, man?" he asked inquisitively.

Antonio looked up at Kelvin and frowned. A time or two, Kelvin had already arrested Antonio for bar fights, and Kelvin knew that Antonio had a bad habit of starting problems where none needed to be started.

"That asshole hit me, man. I don't know what the hell is wrong with them people. I think they just got a problem against me for nothing," Antonio said.

Kelvin sighed and shook his head. "I don't think you're being honest here, Antonio. You want to tell me about the traffic incident?" Kelvin asked.

Antonio shook his head. "Last night, that chick sprayed me with cerveza and then these two say I tried to hit their camioneta. The light was green, and they start problems. What you would do, man? You are going to let some assholes tell a lie. I didn't do shit to them. They can't drive is the problem," Antonio said. His words were heavily influenced with a Spanish accent, and the two Spanish words were familiar to Kelvin.

"Look, you need to pay attention to the road and not get out cussing people, when you're driving. Here, we call that road rage, Antonio. Now, what's this I hear about an altercation?" Kelvin asked.

"That guy punched me in the face for not liking what I

said. I thought this was a country where you can say what you think, eh?" Antonio asked.

Kelvin sighed. "What do you want to do, Antonio?" he asked. By wording his question this way, he didn't give Antonio the knowledge he could press charges against Aaron, and that was the favor he was attempting to do for Jesse's new employee.

"I don't know, tell those people to stay out of my way, and I will drive more careful." Antonio was already on probation, and he assumed he was going to get into more trouble if he continued arguing about the Jessups.

Kelvin nodded and waved a hand. "Okay, Antonio, that sounds good to me. Get in your truck and go home. I don't want to have to come pick you up, any time soon, you got me?" Kelvin stated. Antonio nodded and stood up to walk to his truck. Quickly, he pulled away, leaving Kelvin to talk to Aaron and Ivy.

"So, what's the deal, Kelvin?" Ivanka asked as he walked over to them.

"Antonio didn't ask to press charges, but I didn't clue him in to being able to, either. Best thing I can suggest is everybody just avoid each other, from here on out. I do need statements from everybody," Kelvin said.

Aaron wiped his mouth and stepped forward. "Look, officer, I don't usually get into trouble like this. I'm definitely not looking to be a troublemaker in a town I just came to, but that guy's got some problems. He's been harassing Ivy here for a while, from what I gather. I was just letting him know that ain't going to fly no more," Aaron said.

"I understand what you are saying, believe me, I do. Antonio's a troublemaker and has been since the day he came here. None of us like the guy, but there ain't much more I can do about everything, at this point." Kelvin turned to Ivy. "Ivanka, you can put a restraining order out on him, if you think you need it. Other than that, I really don't know what else to suggest to you. Do you think he's going to be any more of a problem? If so, I can put a guy down there near the bar to look out for you," he said.

Ivanka shook her head and ran her hand through her hair. "There's no need for all that. I got fired from the bar last night for hosing Antonio down with draft beer. Seems to me that if he just steers clear of me, I won't be dealing with him anymore," Ivy replied.

Kelvin nodded back at her. "Okay, so is everybody happy with the story I got here? Antonio almost plowed into the truck, got out of the vehicle to start yelling and got into this guy's face?" Kelvin asked.

"That would be the gist of the story, Kelvin," Jesse said.

"Okay, and what's your name, kid?" Kelvin directed towards Aaron.

"Aaron Kilpatrick," Aaron replied.

Kelvin jotted the name down and started back to his patrol car. "Okay, y'all head home and rest easy. If I need anything else, I'll be down there," Kelvin stated as he opened the patrol car door.

Ivanka gave a sigh of relief and started back towards the truck. She pulled herself inside and Aaron filed in behind her. Jesse turned the ignition and they headed back to the farm in silence.

6

What's the Story?

T he three of them pulled into the drive and filed into the house to find Margaret busy cooking lunch. As she turned around, she smiled and waved them all to sit at the table.

"Hey, y'all. Have a seat; I'll get you some lunch. I've been cooking ever since y'all left," she said.

Jesse gave a huff and sat at the head of the table, shaking his head. "You're never going to believe what happened today, Margie," Jesse began.

"What do you mean?" she asked as she looked back at Aaron and Ivy taking their seats.

"Antonio just about ran smack dab into the tow truck and caused a big old scene downtown," Jesse explained.

Margaret's eyes widened, and she sat down to hear the story. "Oh, really? How did that happen?" she asked.

"Well, the guy almost slammed into the truck, and I hollered at him. He stopped his Ford in the middle of the road and got out, making threats. Aaron, here, decided to play hero." Jesse chuckled.

Margie glanced at Aaron, confused. "Hero? What did you do, Aaron?" she asked.

Ivanka huffed and lowered her head to the table.

"Well, I got out to try to handle the situation amicably, but that guy wasn't about to hear any of it. He started talking about Miss Ivy really awful, and it upset me." Aaron trailed his words and glanced at Ivy before continuing, "So I punched him square in the jaw. Seemed to me, the man had it coming. Apparently, he doesn't know anything about how to talk to a lady," Aaron said.

The confession was all Margie needed to hear before bursting into laughter. "You mean to tell me you punched the scumbag in the face? And I missed it! Darn," Margie said.

Aaron laughed at her response and nodded. "Yeah, I did and almost landed myself in jail on my first day working for y'all," Aaron said.

Margaret looked at Ivanka and then back to Aaron again. "Ah, I'd have bailed ya out, somehow, kid," she said, laughing.

"If I didn't know any better, I'd think you have wanted that guy to get a knuckle sandwich for a while, Mrs. Jessup," Aaron said.

Margaret gave a nod and winked at Aaron as she stood up. "That old boy needs a good butt whooping, and everybody in town knows it. Just cause I'm an older woman don't mean I don't recognize a troublemaker when I see one. I had half a mind to find him and give him a tongue lashing and slapping for what he has put my daughter through. I can tell already, I'm going to like you, Aaron Kilpatrick. From here on out, you call me Margie. No need for formalities, when you're going to be around all the time. Besides, it makes me feel like an old shriveling up woman, and I'm not quite ready to be put out to pasture just yet," Margaret said.

Ivanka lifted her head and glanced at the clock. "It's about time to feed the horses, don't ya think? I think I'm going to walk down to the barn and get to work on that," she said, walking around the table to exit the kitchen.

Aaron pushed his chair back and nodded at her.

"Mr. Jessup, should I go help her out?" he asked, uncertain.

Jesse yawned and leaned back in his seat.

"Yeah, I think I'm a bit tuckered out. You and Ivy ought to be able to handle the job easily," Jesse said.

Aaron smiled and followed out the door after Ivanka. "Ivy!" He called to her as he quickened his pace to catch up.

"You didn't have to come out here, Aaron. You could have sat to enjoy your lunch. I just needed a breather, ya know," Ivanka said.

Aaron nodded and looked down. "I just wanted to say I had no problem standing up for you today, and I'm really sorry that guy said all those things about you," Aaron said.

Ivanka smiled and turned to walk into the barn. "Yeah, well, I'm used to being called all kinds of derogatory things. It's really just the territory of working the bar," she said.

"You don't seem like the type who would, or should, be working a bar, Ivanka. I mean, you seem like a real nice girl, and I just can't picture someone like you behind a counter in a smoke-filled hellhole like that bar," Aaron said, walking behind her.

"Well, I had to do something. Mama and Daddy were having issues making the bills, and I felt like I needed to help. You know, like it was an obligation I needed to fill. Especially after my brother passed away," she said, grabbing the grain bucket and continuing towards the first stall.

"I can understand what you mean. Is that hose over there the watering hose?" He pointed to a black hose in the corner as he asked.

"Yeah, if you want, you can start watering, and I'll grain them out. Then we can flake them. I was actually thinking of saddling up Duchess and going for a ride, myself," she said.

"Oh, yeah? You got a horse I can follow you on? I'd like to get a tour of the property, the right way," he said as he went for the hose.

Ivanka nodded and turned to dump the grain in the first stall feeding trough.

"Yeah, you can ride Mack. I'll show you the creek at the back of the land, too, if you want. It's where my brother and I used to go swimming as kids," she said with a smile.

Aaron nodded and proceeded to complete his chore quickly.

"Sounds like fun. Guess I ought to get my butt in gear and water these animals so we can go for that ride," he said with a wink.

Ivanka's lips twisted into a delighted smile as she turned to continue down the line in the opposite direction. It was a definite fact that Aaron Kilpatrick was setting himself into the dopamine areas of her brain, and Ivy had to admit she liked it. Probably a lot more than she should have.

After Ivy and Aaron completed feeding the animals, Ivanka took Duchess and Mack to the saddling stalls, where Aaron met her.

"Wow, this is a gorgeous horse," he said as he ran a brush over Mack's back.

Ivanka could tell from his demeanor that he had a great appreciation for the animal, and it was another notch in Aaron's favor. "Yeah, he was my brother's horse. Now, he just kind of sits in the stall or, sometimes, we put him out in pasture, but he doesn't really get ridden often, anymore," she stated.

"Well, I hope I can change that. I'd love to take him out and get him some exercise. Has he ever been in any shows? You could win a pretty penny on him, for sure," Aaron said.

Ivanka nodded in agreement. "Yeah, I know. He hasn't been taken to show for a long time, but he has won a couple blue ribbons. Duchess, here, has quite a few, herself. She doesn't belong to us, though, but I'd love to own her. I had hoped, if I worked long enough, I'd be able to afford to buy her, but so far, no such luck. Kind of disappointing, if you know what I mean, but that's just been the way things have gone for me, it seems," she said, placing the saddle on top of Duchess' back.

Aaron frowned and went for the saddle she had brought out for Mack. "Well, maybe one day, you'll be able to, but at least you get to spend your time with her, right? Time well spent, I'd say. I've always thought horses were a soul-connecting animal. Like they made man realize what he had and all he could gain, by just remembering where he came from. The simple things in life, you know?" Aaron asked.

Ivanka smiled at Aaron and nodded again. "You're a real character, Aaron Kilpatrick. I find it hard to believe you've never had any girlfriends, in all this time. Your granddad must've kept a hard hold on you, but I'd say he raised you right. It's surprising, honestly," Ivanka said.

Aaron looked at her with a perked brow. "Surprising good or bad?" he asked.

Ivanka laughed and finished adjusting the saddle and bridle, before pulling herself up onto the beast.

"Good. It's definitely surprisingly good, Aaron. Impressive, really," she said. "Now, you ready to go for that ride? I don't ride soft, mind you," she told him with a grin.

Aaron nodded and hoisted himself up onto Mack. "Well, how about a race, then, Miss Ivy? Where to?" he asked, grabbing the reigns with a chuckle.

Ivanka laughed and kneed Duchess.

"First one to the pasture wins!" she yelled as Duchess galloped out the door, leaving Aaron and Mack in the dust.

"Well, I'll be a fool for letting a girl get a head start on me!" Aaron called out as he kneed Mack onward. The horse quickly started off after Duchess, galloping towards the field in a hurry. Aaron laughed as he watched the dust flying up in front of him. Ivanka was a hell of a rider, and Aaron was already smiling from ear to ear.

"Hurry your butt up, Aaron!" Ivanka called as she brought her horse to a stop.

Aaron pulled hard on the reigns and shook his head as he laughed. "Girl, you can ride like the wind! I had no hope to get ahead from that." He smiled.

Ivanka nodded and urged Duchess into a slow trot. "I've been riding horses since before I could walk. Goes with the territory, you know? You're not too shabby, yourself, Aaron Kilpatrick," she said as the two of them continued towards the creek.

"Yeah, I guess I'm not. I haven't been riding as long as you have, but I've been riding long enough to know a couple things. This horse you got here is amazing and well mannered. I'm impressed. Who does the training?" Aaron asked.

"Dad used to do most of it, and sometimes, he still does. We get paid more for housing and care than training, nowadays, though. It's just too expensive for most owners to pay for anything more. It kind of makes me sad, to be honest. There are a lot of shows and competitions we used to compete in, but things have really slowed lately. Sometimes, I wonder if the market will ever pick back up again," Ivanka said.

Aaron sighed and bit into his lip. He had to admit this girl was something else, and he really liked talking to her. While he had not had a girlfriend in a long time, and getting one was nowhere in his future plans, Ivy was something to consider, and he knew it. Though he couldn't see where dating the boss man's daughter was the best of plans he had, and he wasn't about to ask her on the first real day they spent any time together. Curiosity got the best of him, though, and he had to know.

"So, do you have a boyfriend, Ivanka?" he inquired.

Ivy looked back and shook her head. "Nope. Haven't had one since I graduated, and he ran off to get some cheerleader in college. There really isn't anyone I've been interested in since," she admitted.

Aaron smiled but remained silent.

Ivanka suddenly came to a stop beside a large weeping willow and dismounted. She took the reins and tied the horse to the tree as she waved back at Aaron. "Come on; the creek's down this way." She winked.

Aaron slid from Mack's saddle and followed her lead, tying the animal to the tree beside Duchess. He continued after Ivanka, who stopped suddenly, as if she was waiting for him to catch up.

"How much property does your parents own out here?" Aaron asked her suddenly.

"It's a hundred and fifty acres even. They've owned it since I was a child. My family has been working this land since the Alamo days, I imagine. Dad inherited it when his parents died, and Mom moved in with him when they got married. I figure I'll be the next person to inherit it, if we don't have to put it up for sale, that is. With how things have been going, I never know what's around the corner. You know what I mean?" she asked.

Aaron glanced at Ivy, and his eyes caught hers for a moment. They steadied upon them to notice she had the most beautiful hazel eyes he had ever seen. They were unique in that they seemed have a bright green ring around the outside with specks of gold and brown towards the center of the iris. Surprised by his enchantment with her features, Aaron immediately pulled himself into reality to begin apologizing immediately. "Oh, I, uh, yeah. I know what you mean. I'm sorry I didn't mean to stare at you like an idiot. Really," he stated in embarrassment.

Ivanka's cheek flushed and she waved him to look forward. There, before them, was the sparkling blue waters of the creek and an autumn scene that seemed to come right from a movie. There were dancing golden leaves flowing from the trees. It was still early in the season, but already the golden hue of the grass seemed to reflect on the silvery water below. Ivanka slid to sit cross-legged on the grass and patted the ground beside her.

"It's no problem, Aaron. Have a seat and enjoy the view. It's really peaceful here," she said.

Aaron slid down to his knees and lifted a rock, before tossing it across the water. It skipped across and landed with a thud on the opposite side of the bank.

Ivy smiled and looked back at him as her hands came to rest behind her back. "So, what is your life plan, Aaron? You intending on staying a ranch hand forever? What's your story?" she asked curiously.

Aaron sighed and glanced at her. "You know, for now, I really don't have a clue. I'm honestly not sure what I want to do anymore. After my granddad passed, I kind of felt like a piece of paper blowing in the wind. Ready to land wherever I could and see what the world would show me. There was a time I wanted to play football, and for a while, I had considered race car driving, but now, I have no idea. I don't really know where I'm going to end up, but I know for now, I am thankful for what I have. Your parents have really helped me a lot, and I intend on working my butt off to help them. To help all of you," he said.

Ivanka gave a nod of understanding and turned back to the water. "So, do you know a lot about engines, then, Aaron?" she asked him.

"Yeah, I know a few things, I suppose. Why you asking me that?" He looked at her, puzzled.

"Well, you know my Datsun's not doing well, obviously. I really don't want to spend all my check on a mechanic. Especially when I really need to be looking for another job to help out around here. I hate not working. I mean, I really had considered, for a while, if I shouldn't call Bud back and beg for that job," she said.

"I don't think you should be working in a place that doesn't look out for you. Especially with that jerk we ran into downtown lurking around there. If I were your parents, I would demand you didn't work there. I mean, hell, I just met you and I'm already feeling as if I should talk you out of it," he said.

"Well, I think you are a really nice person, Aaron, and I appreciate that. I really do. I mean, I really appreciate everything you have done. You didn't have to get into a fist fight with Antonio for my honor, though, but I'm still grateful," she said.

"Well, I suppose I could go look at your truck and see what's going on under the hood. It may still cost a bit, if it's something serious like the head gasket or transmission. Is it a manual or automatic?" he asked.

"It's a manual. My brother said if he was going to teach his sister anything, it was how to drive a stick shift. I knew how to drive a stick before I ever learned to drive an automatic." She laughed.

"Well, your brother was smart then, 'cause it seems to be a lost skill, nowadays. It's really unfortunate that some of those city slickers never learn basic survival techniques." Aaron chuckled.

"I agree with that statement, but I guess being from the great state of Texas means I'm supposed to be a country bumpkin who doesn't know a damn thing about anything but horses and desert!" she stated.

If there was one thing everyone assumed about Texas, it was big hats, guntoters, and Republican voters, but there was a lot more to Ivanka than stereotypes, and Aaron was catching onto that quickly. He smiled and pushed himself up to stand, offering his hand to Ivy as he did.

"Need some help up, Miss Ivy? We could head back to the house and get a head start on looking under your hood. I'd like to see what I'm about to get myself into before it gets too much later," Aaron stated.

Ivanka took his hand and pulled herself up to stand with a smile. She held onto it for a second then realizing she was lingering, she released his palm and strode back towards her horse.

"Sounds good to me, Aaron. We can head back now," she said. They both mounted their horses and began trotting back towards the barn. Ivanka could tell her friendship with Aaron was going to be a decent one, and silently, she said a prayer of thanks to God for supplying her with a friend at the moment she needed one most.

7

Seasons Change

I vy and Aaron stood by the Datsun with grimaces on both their faces. Aaron leaned against the vehicle and muttered beneath his breath, while Ivy shook her head in disbelief.

"I can't believe the transmission went out. That would be just my luck. Unbelievable," Ivanka said, annoyed.

Aaron shook his head and turned to look at her.

"I'm sorry, Ivy. It's not going to be an easy fix. It's going to cost quite a bit of money. If you want, you can use my car to go job hunting till you're able to get things settled. I mean, I am not going to be using it much, with work and home being in the same place. You're more than welcome to keep using it, even when you get a new job. All I ask is that you take good care of it. It's all I have left of my grandfather," he said as he wiped his brow, smearing grease across his forehead.

Ivy shook her head. "I can't do that, Aaron. I mean, it's mighty nice of you to offer, but it just doesn't seem like the right thing to do. If anything happens on my watch, I would feel awful about it," she said.

"No, that isn't going to happen. I believe you can handle

the car and I want to help you. I'm going to work really hard on trying to get your truck back up and running but I know this is going to take some time, and you said you needed to start looking for a job. I don't want you to be delayed 'cause of this. Do you think you can afford a new tranny or do we need to look into a patch up job?" he asked.

Ivy looked up at him in surprise and disbelief. This guy was really turning into Mr. Perfect, if ever the man existed. In the back of her mind, Ivy knew Mr. Perfect couldn't exist but Aaron Kilpatrick wasn't too far from meeting her idea of what he ought to be. She hesitated for a moment as she considered what to say. "I don't know, Aaron. I mean I've got a little money saved but how much do you think this is going to cost?" she asked.

"Well, we need to do some pricing so I can't really say. Is there a junkyard around here anywhere?" he asked.

Ivy nodded.

"Yeah, Jon Littleton has a junkyard about ten miles out, on Hooverton Road. It's like twenty minutes from here. I don't know if he has any Datsun parts, though. I guess I could call the parts store downtown, but we may have to order from Advance or something. If that's the case, we are going to have go to the city. Ugh, why does everything have to go wrong for me at the same damn time?" she muttered.

Aaron looked at her and sighed in disappointment. He hated having to tell her the bad news about her vehicle but he really didn't have a choice. It was either let her know the facts as they were or tell a lie. Aaron wasn't a person who liked telling lies, and he really didn't want to set out on a bad foot with the boss man's daughter.

Ivy gave a sigh and started back towards the house. Aaron took the cue and slammed the hood down, following after her. They both entered the house to find Margaret and Jesse sitting down to dinner.

"Y'all ready to eat?" Margaret asked, glancing up at them as they walked past.

"Uh, no. I really think I need to wash up first, Mrs. Jessup," Aaron stated.

Margie's eyes widened and she gave a nod of agreement once she noticed the grease lining his face, and hands. "I can see that. I'll set your places. Get yourself washed up and come on back to supper," she said with a smile.

Aaron nodded and headed back to the bathroom while Ivy strode to the kitchen sink and began washing her hands.

"Aaron says the transmission blew on the Datsun and I'm going to need to get a new one. It's not going to be cheap and I'm really annoyed. I just can't believe my luck," Ivy said as she turned around to look at her parents.

Jesse gave a sigh, and folded his hands to rest on the table. "Well, that's bad news. I guess we need to head down to the junkyard and see about car parts, then. How's this going to affect your job hunt?" he asked.

Ivy pulled her chair back, and took a seat. "Well, I imagine it's going to put me back some. Aaron offered to let me use his car, though. I don't know if I should do that," she said.

Margaret looked back at her daughter and smiled pleasantly. "I think Aaron likes you or maybe you like him," Margaret stated.

Ivy's mouth fell open and she shook her head in disbelief. "Oh, come on, Mama. I just met this guy. He's just being nice and polite. Don't take everything so seriously," she said.

Margie began to laugh slightly and tilted her head. "Well, it must be I hit a nerve for you to react so defensively! He's a nice boy and easy on the eyes, after all," Margaret replied.

"Mama, he's about to come back out here. Please don't embarrass me like that," Ivy stated. "Daddy, tell her to stop with the teasing like that. I just met Aaron, and I don't want to make him uncomfortable thinking I've got some schoolgirl crush on him or something." The words couldn't have come out of her lips any quicker or in better timing, because just as she shut her mouth, Aaron came around the corner and took a seat at the table.

"Wow, you've done a great job here again, Mrs. Jessup," he said, pushing his chair closer to the table.

Margaret gave a huff and smiled knowingly at her daughter.

"Ivy has told us that her transmission blew, Aaron?" Jesse inquired.

"Yeah, I'm pretty sure that's the problem. I told her she was welcome to use my car since I'll be staying here to help you around the farm. I don't see a point in letting it sit there when she needs to be job hunting, and I know fixing her Datsun is going to take some time," he explained. Jesse looked down at his plate and inhaled deeply.

"Well, Ivy, I think that is a nice offer for him to make. Do you think you can go down to the grocer and see about a cashiering job? Or you might be able to get hired down at the Texaco," Jesse said.

Ivy lifted her fork and began chasing a sweet pea across the plate. She stabbed it suddenly and brought the single green ball up to her lips to pop in her mouth. "I suppose I can use his car and see about both places. I may have to drive to the next town over and see about a job there. I don't know if I am going to get anything here, anytime soon," she stated.

Margaret stood up then and walked over to the refrigerator to extract a gallon of juice. She placed it on the table in front of Jesse and sat back down. "I think you should go down to the grocery store as your father suggested. I really don't think it is wise to waste the gas trying to get a job so far away, you know," Margaret said.

Ivy shoveled some stuffing in her mouth and looked back at her.

Aaron glanced between the two women and then looked back to Jesse with an odd expression. It may have been tension in the air but it seemed that something had upset Ivy, and he was still not sure what it was.

"Am I missing something?" he asked suddenly

Ivy looked up at him and immediately began shaking her head. The fear of her mother making it known she may like him was something she didn't want to come out. While it was true Aaron was good looking, nice, and had a body a woman would drool over, she felt it was way too early for him to get any sort of inkling that she found him attractive. Beneath the table, she kicked her mother's foot and cast a warning side-ways glance at her.

"Oh, nothing but Ivanka worrying herself silly over things she really doesn't need to worry about," Jesse said. He pulled the juice over to him and unscrewed the top. "Anybody want a drink or are we all going to act like weirdoes sitting here at the table?" he asked.

Aaron drew his lip into his mouth and half-frowned.

"Something is off about y'all. I can sense it. Did I do something?" he asked, directing the question towards Mrs. Jessup.

"No, silly boy. You haven't done anything but been a great help and a gentleman. If anything, you are the subject matter of all our conversations lately," Margaret said.

Aaron furrowed his brow and lifted his fork to shovel stuffing into his own mouth.

"Mom, you're really going to make him think we are freaks, you know. Dad, how's about filling my glass, please?" Ivy asked. The dinner conversation was growing more and more uncomfortable by the second. All Ivy wanted to do was finish eating and slip out before something was said that would be downright humiliating.

"Mrs. Jessup, you're going to make this country boy blush

like he hasn't in years." Aaron grinned. Just then, he looked up to catch Ivy's gaze in his own and gave a slight wink. It sent a shudder down Ivy's spine as she looked back at him.

Margaret cast a glance between the two and smiled knowingly. It was as obvious as ever they had chemistry, and if her daughter wasn't going to acknowledge it, Margie was going to make her life a living hell by teasing her every day until Ivy confessed. Yet she refused to say anything just yet. Ivy was right about it not being the right time yet, and Margaret knew everything had its time and its season. It seemed the season for Ivy to find a nice boy to entertain her had finally sprung upon them, and even in spite of the events that had led up to it happening, Margaret was starting to feel she had a reason to look forward to the future. It had all come to be with the emergence of this handsome, chivalrous, and caring young man by the name of Aaron Kilpatrick.

Ivy finally finished eating and dismissed herself with a nod to the rest of the diners. She left the kitchen in a hurry and left her parents to enjoy the rest of their meal with Aaron as their dinner companion. As soon as Ivy was out of earshot, Margaret decided to start talking to Aaron some more.

"So, you went riding with Ivy this afternoon, I saw," she said.

Aaron nodded and lifted a napkin to wipe his lip. "Yeah, Ivy showed me the creek and explained to me about her love of the horses. Told me a little about the history of the farm and land. I guess it was the guided tour of Jessup Farm," he said, smiling.

Margaret grinned and tilted her head. "So tell me about your girlfriend, Aaron. You've got to have somebody somewhere, with those charming manners and pristine good looks of yours," Margaret said with a grin.

Jesse chuckled beside his wife as he started to catch on to

her plan. It was obvious to him that Margie was trying to play matchmaker and he had to admit, he found it a little funny.

"You pry too much, Margie. Give the boy a moment to eat his supper and quit giving him the twenty questions. Darn, doesn't he deserve some of his own privacy?" Jesse asked.

Margaret waved her husband off and kept staring Aaron down. "Well, Aaron?" she asked impatiently.

"It isn't a problem, Mr. Jessup. Mrs. Jessup, I really don't have a lady in my life. I just haven't had the time for it, with everything I've had to do these past few years. That isn't to say I wouldn't like to find a sweet girl to spend my time with. Just haven't found the right one or the opportunity to date anybody. Maybe that will change. I don't really know, right now," Aaron explained.

Margaret gave a nod and contemplated her next question. "What kind of girl is it that sticks out to you, Aaron? I know a few girls around here you could probably spend some time with," Margaret said.

Aaron cleared his throat and brought his glass to his lips to take a drink before he answered the question. "Um, I don't really know if that is a good idea, Mrs. Jessup. I've got a lot of work to do around here with your husband, and I don't really have a type of girl, per se," he said

It was obvious to Jesse that his wife's questions had finally begun to make Aaron uncomfortable and he shook his head, looking back at her. "Margie, you're really starting to get too personal now. Cut the boy some slack. He's here to do a job not fraternize with the girls," Jesse stated.

Margie huffed at him and leaned back against her chair, crossing her arms over her chest.

"You just hush up now, Jesse. I'm trying to help this boy out. He isn't going to spend all his doggone time out their slaving for us, you know. It isn't right for you to think it, either. What's the point of working, if you never do anything enjoyable in life? I'm starting to think you've forgotten what it is like to be young. That is half of Ivy's problem; she isn't ever able to have any fun. Now, Aaron, there's got to be a certain type of girl you like. Every boy has a type or types," she finished.

Aaron looked back at Jesse, who had been effectively silenced by his wife, and shook his head with a chuckle.

"You're a stubborn lady, Mrs. Jessup. I guess I just like a girl who can handle herself. Not too tall or too short. Someone who has personality and loves the country life, just like me. I couldn't date any of those fragile, high maintenance types. They're beyond me, really. I do have a partiality for blondes, and something about baby blue eyes just thrills me to the bone. Like sunshine in a blue sky, I guess," he said.

Margaret grinned. Aaron Kilpatrick had just described her Honey Sunshine to a T, and she knew it.

Jesse shook his head as he realized what Margie was thinking.

"Well, that sounds about like honey sunshine," she said innocently as she winked at her husband.

"Yeah, I guess that is what it should be called. A sweet honey that brightens my day like the sun. Though, it seems I'm never going to find someone like that, anyway," Aaron said.

"Oh, I wouldn't say all that now, Aaron. You may be pleasantly surprised. There are some really pretty blonde girls around here," Margie replied with a coy smile.

"Heh, you trying to hint at something, Mrs. Jessup?" Aaron asked.

Jesse roared with laughter as he noticed the boy catching on to his wife's game.

"Now why would you think that? I'm just trying to encourage you to have a little hope now, Aaron. That's what mothers do, you know," she said.

Aaron looked between husband and wife and shook his

head.

"Well, I don't know about all that, but I'll take your word for it for now. Anyway, that was a great meal but I think I ought to hit the hay. Work comes early in the morning," Aaron said.

"Hey, Aaron, you going to head out to the junkyard with me in the morning to see about getting Ivy a tranny?" Jesse asked as Aaron pushed his chair back and started towards the door.

"Oh, yeah. I definitely want to get a head start on seeing about that. What's the morning plan, boss man?" he asked curiously.

"I will let you know in the morning. Be up about six, all right? I want to get out and back before too late. I'd like to get started on getting the harvest list going. We've got to get these fields drawn up before it gets cold. There's a lot to do," Jesse stated.

Aaron nodded and turned to walk away, leaving Jesse and Margie to their lonesome.

"You trying to play matchmaker, Margie? I'm sensing you want to see Aaron take Ivanka out. You know it isn't a very good idea to get our new employee involved with our daughter. Especially when we just met the kid. You're putting way too much pressure on both of them," Jesse stated.

Margie shook her head in disagreement and glanced down at her barely touched plate.

"I disagree, Mr. Jessup. He described his type as exactly what my little girl looks like, and I can tell Ivanka likes him. It's more obvious than your love of bacon and grits," she said.

Jesse chuckled and slid his hand over to rest on top of his wife's. "Honey, you know, sometimes, you need to just let things work in their own time and season. If you force it, it won't grow how you want it to," he said.

"Well, that may be true, but if we leave it up to these kids, they're just going to mess around and never tell the truth. It should be really obvious he likes her, and she definitely likes him. I don't see how it isn't obvious as day to the both of them," Margie said.

Jesse shook his head and gave her hand a squeeze. "Come on, love. Let's get to bed. Day comes quickly and I'm tired from all the drama we endured today," he said, releasing her hand and stepping away from the table.

"I'll be in to bed shortly. I've got to get this kitchen together. I guess you're right. I just hope Ivy starts looking for a way to live herself a life. I don't want to see another of our children's chances taken away before they ever get to enjoy anything," she stated solemnly. Jesse exited, and Margie walked to the sink. Margaret had a terrible time accepting her son's death. He had been a star athlete and a wonderful student. After she got the call he had been killed in the sandbox, she had no idea how to handle her grief. Margie had never expected she would bury her own child, and now, she was starting to feel as if Ivanka had been lost the same day Brenton had been buried. If there was one thing for certain, Margaret wasn't about to let her only living child accept a life of emptiness and work as her only legacy. While she couldn't force Ivanka to date anyone, she could use the opportunity presented to encourage her to go after this chance. A chance that fate had seemingly dumped into the Jessups' laps and one that Margaret knew had to be ordained in the heavens. In that instance, she made a decision. She would play matchmaker better than she ever had in her entire life, and she would help convince her daughter that her interest in Aaron Kilpatrick was a wise one. If Margaret had dreamt up a man for her daughter, it would have been one just like this one, and that was something a mother knew better than to let pass her by. Margaret grinned like the Cheshire cat and began washing the dishes furiously as the gears of her mind began turning.

8

Work, Work, And Work

The next morning, Aaron strode into the kitchen to find Ivy sitting at the table by herself. Shocked, he looked at the clock and leaned into the doorframe.

"Where's your dad, Ivy? I thought we were supposed to get an early start," he said.

"Dad's in the shower, and Mom decided to go feed the horses this morning. She said to help yourself to the food on the stove or some coffee, if you want," Ivy said.

Aaron walked over to the dish strainer and extracted a clean plate. "Your mom always cook such good breakfasts?" he asked curiously.

"Yeah, she is something of a queen of the kitchen. She always has been. She used to compete in baking competitions and things like that. Of course, she hasn't done anything like that since Brenton passed away," Ivy said.

Aaron began forking food onto his plate and sat down beside her. "Your mom took that really hard, didn't she?" he asked.

Ivy nodded and sighed. "Losing my brother was something none of us expected, and it cut deeply. To tell you the truth, I don't think we've gotten over it yet," she said.

Aaron frowned and looked down at his plate before taking a seat. "I hate to hear that. Your mom was telling me she thinks I should start dating somebody around here. Do you know any of the girls she may set me up with? I'm kind of dreading it, to be honest," he said.

Ivy looked up at him and frowned. It disappointed her that her mother was already considering hooking Aaron up with someone else. Much to her surprise, she found it a bit unsettling that her mom would do that, after what she had insinuated the night before. A look of perplexity took over her visage. "Um, I can't say I do. Mom knows a lot of girls down at the church, though." Ivy was unnerved by the admission, and somewhere in the back of her mind, she was even a bit jealous.

"Oh, well, I hope she doesn't send me on some blind date with a girl I will ending up hating," he said.

"What type of girl did she say she was going to set you up with?" Ivy inquired.

Aaron chuckled as he remembered how Margie had worded it the night before. "She said something about a honey sunshine, 'cause I told her I liked pretty blondes with bright blue eyes," he admitted.

Ivy's mouth fell open, and she suddenly looked like she had just seen a ghost. "A honey sunshine?" she asked, to clarify what he had just told her.

"Yeah, you know, like when the sky is so brightly filled with sun that it seems to glow like honey? A clear blue sky?" he asked.

Ivy gave a nod of understanding but shook her head immediately afterward.

"Really, did my mom say anything else about that?" she asked.

Aaron shook his head innocently, and Ivy chuckled in disbelief. "Nah, she didn't say a word about anything else, but I got the feeling she was thinking something she left out. Made me feel kind of awkward, to be honest, but anyway, that's how I always feel when people offer to hook me up with some stranger," he confessed.

"Yeah, I can relate to that. So, you going to let me get those car keys of yours so I can try to find myself a job today?" she asked with a smile.

Aaron gave a nod and reached into his pocket to toss the keys onto the table. "There you go, Miss Ivy. Take care of my baby there, all right," he said.

"Sure thing, captain," Ivy said, grabbing the keys and standing up. She waltzed behind him and continued towards the door before pausing to admit what she hadn't told him, "Ya know what my nickname is, Aaron?" she asked innocently.

"Ivy, short for Ivanka," he said, looking back at her.

"That's one. The other is Honey Sunshine." She chuckled and exited quickly, leaving Aaron to consider what Margie had really meant.

"Wow," Aaron said with a chuckle. He was now beginning to follow the dots, but Ivanka hadn't admitted she liked him just yet. Though Aaron found himself blushing in surprise and secret hope that maybe she did. Truth be told, Ivanka Jessup was a gorgeous young woman, and he was really starting to enjoy her company.

Jesse entered the kitchen just then and sat down in his usual seat. "Ivy already leave?" he asked.

Aaron nodded and looked back at his boss. "What did Margie mean about honey sunshine?" he asked curiously.

Jesse shook his head and looked down at the table. "Let me guess—Ivanka told you her nickname, huh?" he asked in response.

"Yeah, she just did, after I asked her about Mrs. Jessup acting like she wanted to play matchmaker," he said.

Jesse chuckled and patted the table. "Come on, Aaron. Let's get the day started. The junkyard opens in about twenty minutes. Let's see if we can get out there and back in a couple of hours," he stated, turning to walk out the door.

Aaron quickly shoveled the rest of his food into his mouth and rushed to put the plate in the sink. He followed out after the boss man in haste.

Ivy had already pulled out onto the main road and was headed into town. The stoplight where the incident had occurred with Antonio the day before turned red just as she pulled up to it. She frowned and began tapping her fingers against the steering wheel. Her body language gave away her nervousness, and looking from right to left, she stared at the many town shops, wondering who may be able to give her a job. Her eyes finally rested on the diner, and much to her surprise, she noticed a *Help Wanted* sign posted in the corner. The sign hadn't been there the day before, and Ivy grinned as the light turned green. She pulled up to the restaurant and stepped out of the car. Aaron's vehicle handled nicely, and she suddenly felt a great deal of gratitude. She muttered a thank you to God and gave a nod before walking towards the diner entrance. Once she strode inside, she noticed there were only five patrons eating breakfast. It was still early, though, and Ivy knew the place was regularly inhabited by the town's folk on a daily basis. She crossed over to the cash register and smiled as a salt and pepper haired waitress sauntered over to her.

"Morning, sugar. You looking to order a takeout meal?" she asked.

Ivy shook her head and nodded towards the sign in the window. "I noticed y'all are looking for some help. I'd like to apply for the job," Ivy stated. The woman gave a nod and turned to walk towards the kitchen.

"Let me go get the boss and let you talk to him. We just lost our night waitress," the woman explained.

Ivy gave a nod and smiled as she took a seat at the counter. A few minutes later, a chubby older man came around from the back. He approached Ivy with a sheet of paper in his hand and slid it over to her.

"You got any experience in serving, young lady?" he asked.

Ivy's eyes drifted to the paper and she noticed the words, *Application for Employment*, across the top. She looked back up at the man and gave a nod.

"Yes, sir. I've worked as a bartender in the past, but I'm trying to find a more tolerable crowd to serve now. That got a little bit too rowdy for my liking," she said. Ivy figured it was best to be honest, at this point, and start out on the right foot with her would be new employer.

The man looked her over and pointed at the application. "Tell you what, fill that out, and tell Lucille here when you're done. I'll come out and give you an on the spot interview. I really need to get somebody in here as soon as possible. It's hard to run the kitchen and the front line when you're down to four employees from your usual seven," he stated.

"That sounds good, sir. By the way, my name is Ivanka Jessup. It's nice to meet you," Ivy said as she rose from the seat and offered her hand.

The older man gave a nod and smiled. "Well, nice to meet you, too, Miss Jessup. My name's Mike Faraway. I look forward to talking to you more, later." He shook her hand with a firm grip and turned to walk away. Ivy smiled and sat back down.

"Excuse me?" she said.

The waitress who had first spoken to her turned to look at her with a perked brow. "Something I can help you with, honey?" she asked.

Ivy pointed at the application and gave a nod. "Yes,

ma'am. I need a pen so I can fill this out, if you don't mind." She smiled.

The woman pulled a pen out of her apron and handed it to her. "Get it filled out quickly, honey. He will probably hire you and have you start as soon as possible."

Ivy grinned. It seemed luck may have been turning her way, finally, and she furiously began the process of filling out the application. After about ten minutes, she had the entire thing filled out and looked up to motion towards Lucille.

"I'm finished with the application, ma'am," she stated.

Lucille waltzed over to her and glanced down at the paper as Ivy lifted it up to her. "Just sit tight and let me go get the boss," Lucille said, turning to walk back towards the kitchen with the application in hand.

Ivy waited in silence. Her nerves were beginning to get the best of her and all she could hope was that things would go as she needed them to. Just then, Mr. Faraway came around the corner with her application in hand.

"All right, Miss. Jessup. Looks like you've been working in service for a couple of years, now. Mind if I ask you a few questions?" he inquired.

Ivy nodded in agreement. "Of course, anything you like," she replied.

Mr. Faraway sat down in front of her and began reading over her application again. "So, how do you feel about unruly customers?" he asked.

Ivy exhaled and looked back at him. "Well, I feel they shouldn't be allowed to make a scene or disturb the peace of a business establishment. People come out to restaurants to enjoy a decent meal and get a chance to be served. They don't come out to have to deal with nuisances or be upset by somebody else who doesn't know how to act right in public," Ivanka responded.

Mr. Faraway gave a nod of agreement. "So, what do you think a business should do to avoid that?" he asked next.

"Well, if it were my business, I would toss the people out and ban them from my property."

He gave a nod and looked up at her. "Well, you definitely have all the bases covered, Miss Jessup. I think you are hirable. When do you think you can start?"

"Well, I would start today, if possible, but I think I need to get myself prepared for working here," Ivy said.

Mr. Faraway pursed his lips. "Well, how about you come in tomorrow morning, and we get you set on training. Then, you can start coming in to work the night shift."

Ivy smiled and stood up. "That sounds great. What time do you need me here tomorrow?"

He looked at his watch and thought for a moment. "How's about eight in the morning?"

Ivy gave another nod. "Sounds great. Thank you very much, Mr. Faraway."

Mr. Faraway smiled and turned to walk back towards the kitchen.

Ivy walked out the door with an appeased grin playing upon her lips. She couldn't believe her luck. It was as if fate had finally thrown her something to look forward to. Would it continue on the way it was or was something else going to bring her newfound joy to a crushing end? If only she had known, but as the saying goes, news comes in threes.

9

Announcements

J esse and Aaron pulled up to the junkyard and filed out. They were both in great moods and had enjoyed their morning commute and conversation. Neither Margie or Ivy were mentioned; the boys talked about sports and hunting—things they both agreed on and enjoyed. To Jesse, it was almost like having a new son to talk with, and Aaron really liked having an older man to discuss things with again. It was as if destiny had taken from them something they were now finding in each other. They walked across the yard and entered the office with smiles.

"Morning, " Jesse began. "I'm looking for a transmission for my daughter's Datsun. Y'all got any of those around here?"

The man sitting at the desk gave a shake of the head and murmured.

"Nah, we ain't got any Datsuns out in the yard. I haven't seen any in a good while, to tell ya the truth. You might want to try looking at some of the yards in the city or call a parts store."

Jesse looked back at Aaron with a frown.

"Well, what about pull apart yards?" Aaron asked suddenly.

"Pull apart yards? I ain't ever heard of those," the man said.

Aaron nodded. "Yeah, where they have old bodies and you go out on the yard to pull it off the cars, yourself. Mighty popular in the San Antoine area," he stated.

Jesse looked back at the man and nodded. "Well, I guess we'll be on our way, then. Thank you anyhow," he stated, turning to walk back out the door.

The man at the desk murmured behind the two of them, "Yeah, sure."

Aaron got the feeling he wasn't telling the truth about the pull apart lots, and it unnerved him to think what may have caused him to decide to lie. He couldn't prove it, though, so he shook off his suspicions.

"I never did like that guy," Jesse confessed as they approached the truck.

"How come?" Aaron inquired.

"Something about him just doesn't sit right with me. I always get the feeling there's something odd about him. Back here in these woods, he doesn't ever really come to town. I always smell weird things when I come out here. Sometimes, I think he might be into drugs. Can't say for sure, but I just get a really odd feeling off the guy," Jesse said.

Aaron pulled himself into the truck and buckled his seatbelt. "Well, I guess we got bad news to tell Ivy," Aaron said.

"Oh, Ivy Renee` will be all right. My daughter's a strong one, just like her mama. I know she can handle more than she lets on," Jesse said, reversing the vehicle and pulling back out onto the road.

"That her middle name? Well, I reckon I'll have to start looking for a way to get her this part. I'm kind of disappointed. I'd hoped I could get started on her truck before too much longer," Aaron said, looking out the window.

Jesse turned the dial on the radio and focused on the road. "We'll get it, son. Don't worry. We'll get it," he stated again with a nod.

Back at the farm, Ivanka pulled up to the house with a shit-eating grin plastered across her face. She slammed the door and hurried into the house, calling for her mother as she closed the front door.

"Mama! Mama, where are you?" she hollered as she started towards the kitchen.

As usual, Margaret was standing at the sink, and the aroma of something sweet wafted through the air.

Ivy smiled, and walked right inside. "Mama, I got some great news to tell you!" she exclaimed.

"Wow, Ivy, I hadn't expected you back so soon. What's the news, honey?"

Ivy smiled and held out both of her hands as she announced her news. "I got a new job! Down at the diner. I start tomorrow!" she squealed.

Margaret's lips spread out into a pleased grin, and she walked towards her daughter to pull her into a strong embrace. "That's fantastic, Ivanka! I am so proud of you, darling," she said as she hugged her tightly.

Ivy grinned and hugged her mother back. "Isn't it? Maybe my luck is about to change. I certainly hope so."

"Well, you are a good girl, Ivanka. Things have to turn for the better, sooner or later. What time do you have to be at work tomorrow?" she inquired.

"Eight o'clock in the morning. I'm supposed to start training, but he says I will be a regular on the night shift. I'm really looking forward to it, to be honest. Not working just doesn't seem right to me. I feel out of place. You know what I mean?" she asked.

Margaret smiled and gave a knowing nod. "Of course, you're used to making your own money and doing what you want to do. That kind of independence turns real sour when a person loses it. Trust me, I understand," she said.

Just then, they heard the sound of the front door slamming, and after a few seconds, Jesse and Aaron came around the corner with frowns on both their faces. Ivanka tilted her head and watched as Aaron took a seat at the table.

"Afternoon, ladies," Aaron said as Jesse sat down at his end of the table.

"Afternoon. Jesse, Ivy's got an announcement to make," Margie replied.

Jesse turned his attention to his daughter and waited.

"Well, I got a new job today, Daddy." Ivy smiled.

Jesse looked at her and grinned. "Oh, yeah, where you going to work?" he asked.

Ivy went into the explanation about the diner and when she would start.

It was now the time for Jesse and Aaron to make their announcement to her. "Well, that's great news. Unfortunately, Aaron, and I have some bad news to give to you."

"Bad news?" Margaret asked.

Jesse nodded and proceeded to explain how things had gone at the junkyard. A few minutes later, Ivy and Margie were frowning in disappointment.

"Well, the good news is you can still use my car for working down at the diner, Ivy. I'm going to do my best to start looking around for places to get the part you need, and I'm hoping we'll be able to get things going for you, real soon," Aaron stated.

Ivy's face was blank as she listened to Aaron trying to give her a pep talk. "Well, I'm going to try to focus on the good news and deal with the fact that there isn't much I can do about the bad news. Thank you for letting me use your car,

Aaron. I'm really grateful. More than you know," she said, looking across the table at him.

The air was full of their chemistry, and once again, Margie was sensing that her daughter and this boy could have something serious, something she hoped would make Ivanka happy as she deserved to be. The day had gone as best as it could, and in retrospect, it seemed that was all the Jessups could ask for.

Aaron looked down at his plate and a red singe filled his cheeks. He was really starting to like Ivanka Jessup, but telling her was the one thing he didn't know how to do. He had never been one who knew exactly how to ask a girl out, and in the back of his mind, he feared her rejection. If he asked Ivanka out and she said no, he would have to deal with seeing her every day. That wasn't something Aaron was prepared to endure. A man had to have a sense of pride, right? Aaron Kilpatrick wasn't any different than any other man, and a wound to his ego was something he wasn't about to face. Little did Aaron know, but fate was about to toss another wrench into the mix, and the damage was going to be more than he or the Jessups could bear. At that moment, everything seemed perfect, but as life always goes, something was going to disrupt their perfect world. It would all begin the very next day.

10

A Dish Best Served Cold

Ivy had been on the job for three days now, and she was about to begin her first night shift. She pulled her white t-shirt over her body and fastened her black tennis shoes. A quick glance over in the mirror and she was happy to see she was in perfect shape and uniform to work the evening crowd. She applied a thin layer of gloss to her lips and headed out the door. She crossed the living room and leaned into the kitchen to tell her mom she was headed out for the night.

"I'll see you later, Mama, got to go get those tips!" she called, slipping out quickly and heading towards the door. She skipped across the yard and slid into the car with ease. In no time, she was headed back down the road towards town and happy to work again.

Within moments, she pulled up at the diner and walked inside. Already, there were several patrons sitting down to eat. Ivy smiled at each she passed and continued on towards the back to clock in. Mr. Faraway was in the kitchen helping the cook with meals. He winked at Ivy, who then walked back to the front and immediately took over her first table. She strode over to a young blonde and her companion, a little girl about six-years-old. "Welcome to Faraway Diner, I'm Ivy. What can I get you two tonight?" she asked with a smile.

The woman looked up at her and gave a nod towards her menu. "How is the grilled chicken club sandwich here?" she asked.

Ivy looked down at the picture and smiled. "It's actually really good. Before I worked here, I ordered that one a lot. Can I get you two something to drink?" She went on with the usual conversation and finally got the order. She went back to the kitchen and posted it on the turn wheel before waltzing towards the back.

Mr. Faraway caught her halfway and nodded to the garbage cans. "Ivanka, do you think you could take them out for me? Your tables are covered, as usual, but I'm swamped with cooking, tonight. They really need to be taken out, like two hours ago," he said.

Ivy grinned and gave a nod before turning towards the trash bins. She pulled the bags out and eased herself out the back door.

Suddenly, the sound of a Spanish accent filtered into her ears. "Well, hola, senorita," the voice began.

Ivy turned around to face Antonio. Her mouth widened, and she narrowed her eyes in anger. "What the hell do you want, Antonio?"

Antonio didn't give Ivy the answer she was looking for as his lips twisted into a wicked grin. Suddenly, arms wrapped around her waist and pulled her away from the back door. A hand clamped down over her mouth and began dragging her towards the back alley. Ivy struggled against her captor, but she couldn't see him. Antonio walked towards her, extracting a shiny blade from his pocket.

"Mamacita, I told you I was going to have some of that sweet ass, one way or another. You pissed me off, and Luis and I want to try that American bizcocho you got there." The words were laden with hatred and Ivy's heart filled with terror. The man who held her pulled her back towards the Ford Ranger then everything went black.

Ivy awoke to find herself in the center of a large room. All around her were empty beer bottles and fast food wrappers. She struggled to sit up but found she was tied down to the bed. All of her clothes had been torn from her body and all that remained were her bra and panties. As far as she could tell, she had not yet been violated but as she listened closely, she heard the familiar sound of Spanish.

"The bitch deserves it, ese! We should take her down to Tijuana and sell her to the cartel rings. She's a pretty girl. I bet they would enjoy passing her ass around," one voice spoke.

Ivy couldn't recognize the voice but hearing these words was petrifying. She didn't even know if the people who had her were even the ones who had taken her in the alley. What was going on, and why was it happening to her? Ivy's breath caught in her throat, and she felt the sting of tears filling her eyes. A shadow crossed the wall, and she closed her eyes as she awaited the inevitable. Antonio strode over to her and looked down at her body. Ivy's eyes flew open to rest upon his countenance.

"Ah, so you are awake now, eh? You ready to have some fun, Ibanka?" Antonio asked.

Ivy stared back at him in horror as he slid that same blade from his pocket. He inched the knife towards her cheek and slid the blade over her flesh. Ivy's eyes widened in fear and shock. What resided within Antonio was a monster she had never expected. She closed her eyes and struggled against her binds as he brought the blade down towards the middle of her bra. With a snap upward, he slit the bra in two and her creamy breasts fell free. The mounds were perky and immediately bounced against the air as the brassiere snapped. Antonio grinned like a fiend as he brought the knife down to slide into the valley between her breasts. He drew the blade down further still, directing it towards her navel. Ivy grimaced and shuddered in fear as he continued to draw the knife down her abdomen. She began shaking her head furiously.

"Oh. What is wrong, Ibanka?" Antonio inquired as he paused. The blade rested just above her pelvic bone where her panties began. Ivy's right leg began to tremble and she held no control over what her nerves caused. Fear seized her in a vice grip and she stared blankly up at Antonio. With her mouth gagged, she could not respond, but the look of fear in her eyes was all the answer Antonio needed to encourage his devious plans. "Ju don't worry about nothing, Ibanka. I am going to take burry good care of you. I promise. Yes, I am going to really take care of ju, and this sweet little cuerpecito of jurs," he said. He drew the blade down to slice the frilly lace of her underwear in one quick motion. Ivanka struggled to close her thighs as the man's gaze steadied upon the mound of hair that rested between her supple thighs. She had no control over what was about to happen to her, and the realization that nobody was coming to save her or that no one would expect her home for hours made her begin to panic. The blades of the knife bit into her skin as Antonio drew it further down her body. Slowly, he drew the knife down her thighs. It was almost as if he was attempting to continue the torture at such a slow pace that she would begin to grow weak from the petrifying fear alone. His method was working fantastically, and Ivy immediately balled up her fists until her nails cut into the palms of her hands.

"Just as sweet as I thought you would be, Ibanka. I wonder how your center will taste. Is it like honey, mamacita?" he asked. He dropped the blade onto the floor and pulled himself on top of her. She could feel the throbbing heat of his erection against her thigh as he breathed into her face. The putrid stench of his breath singed her nose and he brought his hand up to caress her cheek. It was a disgusting attempt at affection and Ivy grimaced and trembled in response. Her heart began to beat furiously within her diaphragm and she kicked her feet against the footboard. Antonio leaned forward and pulled the gag from her lips with his teeth. In an instant, his mouth was upon hers and Ivy instinctually reacted by biting his lower lip

"Do you believe in Jesus, Ibanka?" he screamed and spat in her face. The sting of his spittle flew into her eyes and Ivy sobbed in terror. He had yet to rape her, but already she had been violated.

11

Intimidation Game

A few hours later, she awoke with a splitting headache and bruises up and down her body. Antonio was no longer in the room. Ivy found herself gagged, once more, and unable to speak. The cool autumn air fanned out across her nude and bound body, causing goose bumps to rise all across her alabaster skin. She was nearly freezing and it added to the torment she already felt. Agony was the only word she could think of at the moment. A brutalizing terror had gripped her, and it was far from over. It surprised her that Antonio had yet to rape her fully, but she knew that the time for that was not far off. She shivered, suddenly, and attempted to close her eyes, praying that sleep would overtake her again. She made a silent plea to God for someone to go looking for her soon. The only hope she had was in Mr. Faraway noticing she had not come back from throwing the garbage out, but she didn't even know where she was. For all she knew, Antonio could have driven her across the border into Mexico, and she may never be able to see her family or town again. Horrors continued to fill her mind as she contemplated the many variables that could present themselves in this situation. There were so many different possibilities and so few answers. She shivered again and groaned, against her better judgment. She didn't really want her captor to come back into the room anytime soon, but at the same time, she was shivering almost violently from the cold. Her body yearned for some comfort. A blanket or even a sheet would have been a welcomed gift at that second. Her lips had already begun to take a blue shade from the cold. Ivy relaxed her wrists in their bindings and struggled to ease her breathing as she focused on the ceiling above her. The sound of a voice behind her alerted her to someone else having entered the room. Once more, a petrifying fear overtook her and Ivy shook her head as if to say no.

"Are you cold?" a woman's voice asked softly.

Ivy shockingly looked to the side to spot a young Hispanic girl no older than fifteen, at max. Ivy looked over her confusedly, but the girl approached with a knitted poncho. Gently, she spread it across Ivy's body and gave a half smile before turning to walk away. Ivy was really confused now. She had no idea where she was or who resided there, but thinking young girls were in the same building made Ivy fear it may have been a makeshift prostitution ring. With her head swimming, she closed her eyes and forced herself to drift off into a light slumber.

Midnight rolled around and Ivanka had still not come home. Margie had been sitting up watching late night TV, hoping her daughter would make it in before she got too tired. She wanted to hear all about her first night on the shift for which she had been hired. Margaret glanced at her husband, asleep on the couch, and pursed her lips. There was something about mother's intuition that led Margie to believe something wasn't exactly right. She stood up and glanced at her watch just to make sure, before walking to the window to peer outside. The car still hadn't pulled up, and Margie frowned unpleasantly.

"Jesse, Ivy still isn't home, and it's after midnight," she said.

Jesse didn't even stir from his sleep, and Margie turned around, raising her voice, "Jesse! Wake up!"

Jesse shifted and cracked an eye to look back at his wife. "What are you hollering' at me for now, woman?" he asked, annoyed.

Margaret nodded to the clock on the wall. "It's past midnight and Ivy isn't home yet," Margaret said.

"Have you tried calling her yet? Maybe she got caught up cleaning the diner or something," Jesse said, completely unaffected by his wife's statement.

"No, but she should have been here, by now."

"I think you are just worrying yourself over nothing again, woman," he stated, rolling back over on the couch.

Margie frowned and walked over to the phone. She dialed Ivy's cell and let it ring a few times.

"*Hi, you've reached Ivy's phone. I can't take your call right now, but if you leave me a quick message with all the details I will be sure to call ya right back when I can! Have a great day!*

Ivanka's voicemail came on. Margie groaned and left a message.

"Ivy it's your mom. I'm worried about you, honey. Is everything all right? It's a quarter after midnight, and you're still not home. Give me a call and let me know what is going on. I love you, sweetheart," she said, hanging up the phone. She paced back over to the TV and turned to walk back to the window.

Jesse had begun snoring by this point, and Margaret frowned in disapproval. "Jesse, wake up! I am serious. Something's not right, and I can feel it," she said with a worry-laden tone.

Jesse didn't flinch, and Margaret decided to give the diner

a call. She sat down to begin raking through the phonebook hurriedly and finally came across the number. Once more, she lifted the receiver and furiously began dialing the number. The phone rang and rang, but nobody picked up. On the tenth ring, Margie finally decided they must've already closed up shop and maybe Ivy had her phone again. She hung up and redialed Ivy's cell. Again, the sound of Ivanka's voicemail filled her ears. In frustration, she slammed the phone down and walked over to the window. As she looked up at the barn, she noticed that Aaron's lights were still on, and she peered back at her husband. In an instant, she made the decision to go out the door and walk across the yard towards the barn. In a hurry, she jogged up the stairs and began pounding on his door.

Aaron came to open it with a shocked look on his face. "Um, everything alright, Mrs. Jessup?" he asked with a perplexed look on his face.

Margie shook her head and frowned. "Have you heard from Ivanka? She still isn't home yet, and I tried calling her twice. I also called the diner and there was no answer. I'm really getting worried," she stated.

Aaron looked at her and immediately shook his head. He waved to Margie to enter the apartment, and sat down. "Maybe she stopped at a gas station or something. What did Jesse say?" he asked. At this point, all Aaron could think was that Margaret was freaking out over nothing, and he needed to calm her down.

"Jesse's asleep, and he thinks she is probably just held up at work. I don't think so, though. I called the diner and it rang and rang. She didn't answer her phone, either. That is not like Ivy, at all," Margie stated.

Aaron could tell Margaret wasn't about to have rationalization used against her. "Well, let's not start thinking the worst, just yet. Let's wait a few more minutes and give her the benefit of the doubt, okay?" Aaron said.

"I'm worried. How am I supposed to just sit tight and ignore that? My daughter never does stuff like this. I think we ought to call the police," Margaret said.

Aaron shook his head in disagreement. "I think it is a little too soon to be calling the police, Mrs. Jessup. Ivanka is a grown woman, and I believe there is a twenty-four-hour missing limit before the cops can even do anything. By the time you get them interested in looking for her, Ivy will already be home. I'm sure of it. Try not to get so bent out of shape over her coming in late. I think you raised your daughter up right, and I think she can handle her own. Don't sweat the small things, Mrs. Jessup." He looked at her and continued, "I know you've lost a child, and I can't say I understand how that feels. I do understand how it feels to lose someone you love, though, but we can't let our grief cause us to become consumed with fear and worries. I'm sure Ivanka will be fine and home in no time," Aaron reassured her.

Margaret looked back at him and sighed. It was impossible to explain a mother's intuition to a man. It was just something they didn't understand, but in the back of Margie's mind, she knew something wasn't right with Ivy. She may not have been able to prove that to Jesse or Aaron just yet, but in her heart, she knew something was amiss, and she was dead set on finding out what it was.

"I really hope you are right, Aaron. At least you are trying to console me here. That is more than I can say for Mr. Jessup's lazy bum," Margie stated

Three hours later, Ivanka had still not come home. Margaret had moved back to the house and tried calling the diner and her cell, several more times. There was no answer. Aaron sat across from her on the loveseat. Jesse still snoozed on the couch. As Aaron peered up at the clock on the wall, he felt his stomach begin to grow into knots. His earlier reassur-ances seemed pointless now, and he was starting to think Margie might have been right. He stood up, suddenly, and moved to shake Jesse from his slumber.

"Mr. Jessup, I hate to wake you but it's three o'clock in the morning, and Ivy isn't answering the phone and she hasn't come home yet," he said.

Jesse rolled over and looked up at Aaron, furrowing his eyebrows as he steadied his gaze. He sat up and placed his head in his hands.

"I'm worried to death, Jesse! We need to go looking for her, at least. I told you something wasn't right," Margaret exclaimed from her seat.

Jesse pulled his palms away from his face and looked at his wife. He gave a solemn nod and pushed himself up to stand. "I'm going to head into town and do some looking around. Aaron, you mind staying here to calm the missus. I don't think she's going to do much good looking for Ivy, in her state of mind," he stated.

Before Aaron was able to give an answer, Margaret was on her feet, rushing for her jacket. "I'm not about to stay here while you go looking for her, when I've been the one sitting here waiting for hours. I'm going with you!" she hollered across the room.

Aaron stepped up to the coat rack and pulled her jacket down, holding it out for her to take. "No need to holler at your husband, Mrs. Jessup. You two go on to look for her. I will stay here and wait to see if she shows up. I'll give you a call, if she happens to come home," he said gently. His attempts to calm the lady of the house were met with a huff and a shake of the head.

"No, I don't think that's a wise idea, either, Aaron. The more of us out looking about for her, the more likely we are to find her. I'm telling you, this needs to be a search party. I can feel it in my bones."

Aaron looked towards Jesse and gave a defeated shrug. "What do you think, boss man?" he asked.

Jesse bit into his lower lip and wiped his right eye with his index finger. "I think she's about to lose her mind with fretting like she does. For all we know, Ivanka could have had some more car trouble and got caught up or something. Phone service goes out all over the place. It's nothing too unusual. I don't know why she's got to go and get her panties in a wad," Jesse stated.

Margaret suddenly stormed across the carpet and lifted her right hand to slap him square across the cheek. Her eyes radiated an anger that screamed a woman's wrath. "Now, listen here, Jesse DeWayne Jessup! I've just about had it with you acting like I'm a pain in your big old white ass while I'm worried about our only daughter! I've got every right in the world to worry about my baby girl, and damn it, I'm not going to be undermined by your careless and thoughtless attitude! Get your ass in gear or sleep with the damn dogs tonight. Aaron, let's go!" Margaret ordered.

Aaron stared in disbelief at the scene before him. The sweet and caring Margie had always seemed to be the glue that held the Jessup family together. Aaron never imagined she had that kind of fire in her petite frame. Uncertain of what to say, he looked between husband and wife.

"Uh, yes, ma'am," he finally uttered, following after Margaret.

Jesse lifted his hand to rub his stinging cheek and shook his head with a sigh. It suddenly dawned on him that he was being a certified asshole and he needed to change his tune— real quick and in a hurry like.

"She's right, Aaron. I'm full of piss and vinegar, when I should be out there looking for my little girl. Let's get a move on; the diner opens in an hour and a half. We'll stop by and get some breakfast there and ask Mike what's going on. If we don't find Ivy before then, that is," Jesse said.

Aaron nodded and walked down the corridor towards the front door. Margaret flung the door open and waltzed out the front entrance in haste. The two men followed behind her as quickly as their feet could carry them. In a matter of moments, the three of them were headed down the main road, towards town. It was a silent and awkward drive, the entire way there, and as they pulled up to the main red light, Margie finally piped up.

"Hey, y'all see that? That's Aaron's car, parked right beside the diner, but the lights in the restaurant are off," Margaret stated.

Aaron looked out the window and lifted a brow. "How about you park the truck over here, and we'll walk around the building?" Aaron asked.

Jesse eased the vehicle into an empty space on the side of the road. He put the truck in park quickly and flung his door open. Aaron followed suit, and Margaret filed out behind him. The three of them had perplexity written all over their faces. There was just something too odd about it, and it caused the hair at the back of Aaron's neck to rise.

"Yeah, let me go check out the car first. I want to see if there's something wrong with it or anything," Aaron replied. He jogged over to the car, leaving Margie and Jesse watching in silence. He quickly walked around the car, inspecting it, but found nothing awry in his investigation. As he came to a halt, he pursed his lips and looked back at the Jessups, shaking his head as if to say nothing seemed out of place. Jesse lifted his hand and waved Aaron towards the right of the building. Aaron gave a wave in return and started off towards the opposing side. Margaret and Jesse quickly crossed the street and scouted their end of the edifice. Once they met in the middle, the three them looked more baffled than they had before arriving.

"I just don't understand what is going on here," Jesse said. The car was perfectly fine, and Ivy's job seemed to be in expected usual shape. Jesse looked down at his watch and frowned. There was still another hour before the diner was due to open. He had no clue what time Mike came in to start the morning chores, but he knew it was at least another thirty minutes before anybody showed up. The town rolled up at night, and every shop down the main strip was dark. Jesse suddenly began to feel hopeless and looked back at his wife with a look of sorrow and disappointment. He had no idea what to tell her, but the expression on Margaret's face told him all he needed to know. She was right. Her feeling had been spot on, and something was seriously not adding up. Margie's eyes began to water as she read her husband's face. Where had Ivanka gone, and why hadn't anyone listened to a mother's natural instincts sooner?

12

You're Mine

A ntonio strode into the room where he had been keeping Ivy, with a pleased grin spread across his face. Ivy remained sleeping, with the poncho draped over her nude body. As the man approached, he scanned his victim closely and leaned forward to trail the tips of his fingers over her cheek. Ivy's eyes fluttered open to meet with the man's ugly mug. He grinned wider as he noticed the fear filling her eyes quickly. His fingers gripped the poncho and ripped it from her in a single motion, exposing her body to the cool air once again. Ivy closed her eyes tightly, preparing for the inevitable.

"Are you ready for it, mamacita?" Antonio asked in an icy tone. Ivy pressed her backside into the mattress and bit fiercely into her gag. The fear of being raped had been at the front of her mind since the moment she had discovered herself in captivity. Antonio's fingers shifted to his belt buckle and the jingling sound of metal filled the room. It was an ominous and horrifying echo that seemed to continue, even after he had completely removed the belt. The sound of his pants falling on the floor beside her clued Ivy in that he was about to have his way with her. Grimy fingers found their way between her thighs, and he violently widened them to plunge his body between her legs.

She kept her eyes closed, hoping to chase away the image, silent prayers filling her mind as she tried to imagine it was all a dream—a nightmare she had created in the dead of her sleep. It was no dream, however, and Ivy was made a key player in the event the moment. Antonio released her throat at the moment Ivy was sure she would pass out. Tears slid down her cheeks. She felt helpless, violated, and like a corpse with just enough life in it to be considered near death. Her flesh had begun to turn pallid and ashen. Not the usual sun-kissed pink that had caused her parents to give her the nickname, Honey Sunshine. Ivy looked just like death warmed over but reality was a cruel mistress, and the sound of Antonio's voice filtered into her ears as she fell unconscious yet again.

"Now you are mine, Ibanka. Just like I said you would be," he muttered.

It was now five o'clock in the morning. Aaron, Jesse, and Margaret sat in a corner booth. They had each ordered a cup of coffee and an omelet, scarfing it down as quickly as it was delivered. They now waited for Mike Faraway to come talk to them. Mike strode over to their table and sat down beside Aaron, folding his hands to rest atop the table as he pursed his lips. Mike had no idea what to tell the family, as he, himself, was confused by the entire situation.

"Well, it went about like this; the last time I saw Ivanka was when I asked her to take out the trash, about an hour after she clocked in. She seemed to be in a normal mood and took it out the back door. After that, I didn't see hide or tail of Ivy for the rest of the night. I figured she probably quit, and I was left with another slot to fill. Other than that, I really don't know what is going on, Mr. and Mrs. Jessup," he stated grimly.

Margaret's eyes began to tear up, and she placed her head in her hands.

"Do you know about what time that was?" Jesse asked, casting a side glance at his wife.

Mike sighed. "I guess it must have been about seven o'clock."

Margaret immediately brought her hands from her face as her mouth flew open. "You mean to tell me you didn't see her for the entire night and never got an inkling that something might be wrong?" she accused angrily.

Mike looked at the distraught woman with a frown. "I'm sorry, Mrs. Jessup. I don't know what else to tell you. I mean it seems odd to me, too," he said.

His failed attempt at reassuring her didn't bode well, and Margie pushed her coffee mug away as she stood up. "You're sorry? You should have investigated! You should have let somebody know what the hell was going on when you locked up the diner last night! You could have called or at least paid attention to the fact that her car hadn't been moved! You really think she quit? What did she do, walk off into the corn-fields without anything she owned? Are you dense, man?" Margaret screamed. She was boisterous and angry and each word was lined with an accusatory tone. Though she may not have said it, she was thinking something was off about his supposed innocence.

"Margie, that's enough, now. You and I have known Mike since grade school. You don't mean all this. Mike, you got to give her some slack. You know she had an awful nervous breakdown after Brent passed away," Jesse said, casting a side-ways glance at his wife. It was meant to be a warning to calm her down before the law got called to haul them all out of the diner.

"It just don't seem right to me. How could he just lock up and ignore her car sitting there, after hours of not seeing 'hide or tail' of her, as he put it." Margaret made quotations with her fingers in the air as she said the words.

Aaron was beginning to feel really awkward and scooted towards Mike. "Mind letting me out? I think I need a breather, and I'm going to go down the block to talk to the police. See if anything has been reported, or if anything odd was seen last night," he said.

Mike moved out of the booth and stood up, giving Aaron the space he needed to exit. He looked back at Margaret and shook his head. "Now, Margie, I know you are upset, and I can't say I blame ya. I'll help all I can with trying to find out what happened with Ivy, but you can't go blaming me for expecting a twenty something young woman to just walk out during a shift. It has happened lots of times, and it is a pretty common occurrence," Mike stated.

Margaret shot him a look of pure malice. The more Mike spoke, the angrier she got, and without answering him, she stormed off towards the front door, slamming it in the process as she went outside.

Aaron gave a nod towards the exit and followed out. "That would be my cue to get out the door," Aaron said, leaving Jesse and Mike staring in shock.

Jesse lifted his hand and began rubbing his left temple. This entire ordeal was really starting to get to him, but with Margie's anger mounting, he knew someone had to hold it together. He drew his hand back to his side and shook his head. "I'm sorry, Mike. She's really sensitive about Ivy. Ya know, it's all she has left, and that ain't easy on a mama. I'm sure she will apologize, and don't take it seriously. You aren't to blame. Just ask around. See if your regulars saw or heard anything strange or if anybody has a clue where Ivanka may have gone off to. I'm hoping she just did something stupid and inconsiderate. I'd hate to think of the other possibilities, right now," Jesse stated.

Mike nodded. "Yeah, no problem, Jesse. I just hate to think Margaret thinks I'd lie about anything like this. I've got kids of my own, and I know what it's like to worry sick about 'em. I mean, Matty is going to school up at the University of Texas now, and Hailey's about to graduate. I understand how it feels. Believe me, I can't imagine how upset Belinda would be if something happened to either of our kids," Mike said with a worried expression. The tone of his voice gave Jesse the notion he was telling the truth and that his wife had been entirely too accusatory for her own good. Margaret had fire engine red hair, and she lived up to the saying that redheads were full of piss and vinegar if you pissed them off. Some people said they had no soul, but that was not the case with Margie. Her problem was too much soul and too much pressure in a tiny body. The strength of her character was an impenetrable fortress on most days, but everybody had a limit, and Margie's soft spot had always been her babies.

Aaron walked out the door to find Margie crying like a baby.

"I don't know what to do. I don't know how to help my baby girl or where she is or if she is okay or if she is hurting. I feel like I have completely let my kids down. First, Brent, and now, Ivy! God's got to be pissed at me for something. Oh, my word. Where's my little girl?" she wailed as Aaron took her into his arms. He held Margie there for a minute and began rocking her gently.

"Let's go over to the station and see about a report, all right? See if we can get something going to find her."

"Oh, I look like a wreck. I just can't help it! I don't even know if I can talk to the police or not," Margie stated.

Aaron pulled her hand towards the road and smiled. "Sure, you can, and you need to, so we can find out what's going on with Ivanka. So we can find her." Each hour that passed by, Aaron started to feel more concerned, but now, his fear was something he was doing his best to hide. It wasn't the easiest thing to do, but he knew somebody had to do it. They crossed the road and walked two blocks down the sidewalk to the station. Kelvin was sitting at a desk with his feet propped up when they sauntered into the building.

"Morning, officer," Aaron began as Margie filed in behind him. "We need to file a missing person report."

Kelvin looked up at him and immediately placed him from the incident with Antonio, days before.

"Missing person? Who is missing?" Kelvin asked, pulling his feet down and sitting up to look past Aaron and assess who else had come in.

"Morning, Kelvin," Margie said, folding her arms across her chest and giving a frown. "The missing person is my daughter, Ivanka Jessup."

"Ivy's missing? Wait, let me get the right paper work out for this." He started filing through documents and found a missing person report, in a matter of seconds. Just before he was about to start filling in the name on the page, he halted and looked back up at Margie. "Wait, wait. How long has Ivanka been supposedly missing?" he asked suddenly.

Margie glared at him and pointed at the report. "Fill out the form, please, Kelvin! *My daughter is missing!*" she insisted.

Kelvin looked at her and put both his hands up in a wave. "Now, listen, Margaret. I'm an officer of the law, and this is the police department. You're not going to holler at me like we were friends since grade school, as you usually do when I'm not in uniform. While I am on duty, I demand you respect me as an officer of the peace around here," he stated firmly.

Margie scoffed and shook her head. "Well, ya sure as hell ain't adding to my peace for nothing. Ivy went into work last night at six, and nobody has heard from her since seven last night. The car she used is still parked outside Mike Faraway's diner. Before you ask, we called and called and called again. There was no answer. Ivanka has gone completely missing, and I want to start looking for her straightaway."

Kelvin groaned and put his hands back on the desk.

"Let me explain to you how protocol goes on something like this, Margie; first, she has to be missing for at least a full twenty-four hours. It's ten till six now. That means you got thirteen more hours before I can get this properly filed. Now, I can start filling in the details for when I ready to finish the report, but I can't put out any APBs or anything like that until the twenty-four-hour mark is reached," Kelvin said.

Margie's eyes widened in disbelief. "Twenty-four hours and she may already be dragged across the Mexican border, Kelvin! Can't somebody help me out here? I need to rally people to start looking and investigate where the hell my daughter is!" she demanded.

Kelvin looked at Aaron, who had remained silent for the duration of the conversation. "Young man, do you think you can help get her a rallied party up? I mean, I can go start asking questions and things, but I can't file the report before protocol is up. It's the most I can do. You're really getting bent out of shape here, and for all you know, your daughter could've decided to run off with some guy she met at the diner last night," Kelvin said.

Margie's anger was heightened in an instance, and Aaron noticed her balling her fists at her side just before she went off in a cussing rage at Kelvin.

"You fucking asshole! What you trying to insinuate, that my daughter is a damn whore? She *is* missing, and this worthless crack hole police department isn't going to do shit about it!" she fumed.

Aaron pulled her towards the exit and gave a nod towards Kelvin. "She's just about to have a nervous breakdown, Officer. Please, let me take her back home, and you can go talk to Jesse at the diner. I think he can help you with the details for filling out that form."

If Margie hadn't been who she was, Kelvin would have arrested her for disorderly conduct on the spot. It was to Margaret's advantage that Aaron began urging her out the door. Margaret stormed off across the street and flung the truck door open to pull herself inside. In a hissy, she had made an ass of herself but the men around town were starting to prove to be incompetent jackasses, if ever she had met any.

13

Frantic

Aaron drove Margaret home and brought her into the house. He knew he was going to have to head down to the police station to pick Jesse up soon, but they had both agreed that getting Margie back to the house was the best mode of action. The woman's frantic worry had gotten the best of her and she had insulted both Mike Faraway and Kelvin. Two people whom she usually held a great deal of respect for. Margie was a powerhouse of a woman, but when her attitude took over her brain, she had a tendency to develop a really bad case of 'diarrhea of the mouth.' The pressure of not knowing where Ivy was had built up her frustration, and Aaron was thankful they hadn't been forced to bail her butt out of jail after her scene downtown. Margie sat cross-legged in her recliner with a solemn expression plastered across her face. She was definitely feeling at a loss and had no idea where to start. The hours couldn't be any less grueling, and Aaron gave a sigh as he headed back towards the door.

"Margie, I understand why you are feeling as you do but I think you really ought to get some rest. There isn't anything else you can do for Ivy right now. I know it is killing you to sit there feeling useless. Believe me, I get it. I just pray to the good Lord above, we will hear something soon. Try not to think too much more on it. All it will do is make your stress load that much worse. You sit here and watch a show or something. Take a nap and rest at ease. I promise you, I will help you find Ivy," he said from the door. Margie looked back at him and gave a forced smile. Aaron slid out the door and disappeared from sight.

It had been twelve hours since Antonio had abducted Ivy from Faraway Diner. She had not been given food or water since she arrived. Since she had seen the teenage girl the night before, she became aware that her name was Rosalia. She spoke very little English and seemed scared about Ivy being there. From the little Spanish Ivy knew, she discerned that Rosalia didn't approve of her kidnapping and that Antonio called her hermanita, which meant little sister. Presumably, the girl was his younger sister and that gave Ivy the idea that he had taken her to his house or to a relative's, at least. She didn't know much more about Antonio's family, and the only person she knew him to regularly hang around was Luis.

Rosalia stepped into the room with a tray of food and a pitcher. Ivy couldn't make out what it was but it smelled heavenly, and even though she had not been hungry before, she now had the desire to eat a mountain of food. Rosalia placed the platter on the nightstand beside her and frowned as she looked over Ivy's nude and brutalized body.

"I want to help you, but you cannot scream, okay?" she explained. Ivy feared what would happen if she did and gave a nod of understanding. Rosalia pulled the gag from her mouth and sighed. "I will give you food and water. I can't untie you or Antonio will hurt me, too," she explained.

Ivy nodded and coughed as she attempted to find her voice. "Ahem, thank you," she muttered.

Rosalia nodded and lifted a fork to bring it her lips. "De nada. I'm sorry my brother is hurting you," she said in a sad voice.

Ivy sensed that Rosalia felt guilty about the situation and wondered if she could use it to her advantage. "Do you know why he is doing this to me?" Ivy asked before taking a bite of the offered morsel.

"Hermano says you hurt him first. He says you did something mean and you deserve your punishment," Rosalia explained.

From the way she said it, Ivy deciphered that she did not believe that and it made her feel a moment of false security as Rosalia continued to offer her more bites of food. Ivy swallowed some and opened her mouth again. "How can I make him know I am sorry and make him stop hurting me? How can I take the punishment and make it end so he doesn't have to hurt me anymore?" Ivy asked. In the back of her mind, it infuriated her that this man was telling his adolescent sister she had done something to deserve rape and torture. The depth of Antonio's darkness was even more obscure than Ivy had ever imagined, and it seemed he was trying to rub it off on an impressionable young lady.

"I don't know. I asked him if he would let you go, but he said he couldn't now. He said if he does, you will tell the police and he will get in more trouble because of you telling lies," Rosalia explained.

Ivy could not believe what she was hearing, and suddenly, she felt the urge to begin crying again. "Is he going to kill me?" she asked in a whisper.

Rosalia put the fork down and lifted the pitcher to pour her a glass of water. "I am going to try to persuade him not to. I hope he does not. I do not want my brother to commit murder and have Dios condemn him to Hell," Rosalia said.

Ivy realized, in that statement, that Rosalia was a devout Catholic and her fear for her brother's soul was sincere.

"If he does kill me, will you do me a favor?" Ivy asked suddenly, playing upon the girl's belief system, in the hopes she would help her escape.

"What kind of favor?" Rosalia immediately grew suspicious and her rigidity became apparent as she looked back over Ivy. "Could you go to the Santa Maria Catholic Church and ask for Padre Josue? He is the man who baptized me as a baby, and I would like him to administer last rites or prayers of benediction. Please?" she begged the girl with teary eyes.

Rosalia squeezed her eyes closed for a second and shook her head. "If I tell the Padre, Antonio will get angry at me. I can't do that. Oh, no. Will Dios punish me for his pecados, too?" she asked in a frantic voice.

Ivy sighed and looked to the glass of water. "Can I have a drink now?" she asked sadly. It was not going to be easy to convince this girl to help her. Water and nourishment were essential to keep her strength up.

Rosalia brought the water to her lips and held it there as Ivy drank. "You better rest some more. Antonio is at work now. He will be back soon. You will want to sleep." She pulled the glass from her lips and replaced the gag. After collecting the tray, she walked to the door, pausing as she looked back at Ivy. "I will bring you a blanket. I know it is cold in here," she finished.

Ivy leant her head back against the bed and stared at the ceiling. She could not believe this was happening. It seemed surreal, and the girl seemed to be in the wrong place, being raised by a psychopath. She wondered how many other people lived in the house or if there were other children or elder family members. She wondered if any of them knew she was being held back there or if they were all just as crazy as Antonio was. Luis had not presented himself at all since the kidnapping and Ivy wondered if he would be the next one to violate and torment her as Antonio had done. She found relief in knowing he was at work and prayed he would go down to Bud's that night, instead of coming directly back to her. The words he had spoken to her, just hours before, filtered into her mind as the memories burst into Technicolor in her head.

"Ibanka, you are mine..." Ivy clutched the binds again and bit into her gag ferociously. If she could just get out of the ropes, she could easily get the bowie knife from Antonio. An idea began to take root in her head and she wondered if the old homage of catching more flies with honey rather than vinegar would bode true in the case of Antonio. He had always lusted after her, and it had been his continual advances and her shooting them down that had resulted in this catastrophe. With consideration to the possibility of him killing her, Ivanka knew she had to start plotting and playing her chess moves quickly. The first step had been in attempting to forge a makeshift friendship with his sister, but the next step would be in stomaching the idea of being nice to her violator—the possibility of actually going along with what he wanted. Rebellion had not worked, but maybe, just maybe, giving in to his whims may win her a consolation prize. Ivy had nothing else to lose at this point, and after all, it was her life that was balancing on the line. A game of cat and mouse had been declared, and the key to all wars was knowing one undeniable fact; the art of war was deception. Yet, whose deceiving ploy would prove the better? Ivanka's, or Antonio's? That was a question only time could answer, and as Ivy continued to think out her battle scheme, she drifted back into the dream world,

where everything was just as it always should be, though the dreams she entertained were about another male altogether. The man she knew was fated to be her hero since the first day he ever saw her—Aaron Kilpatrick, Ivy Jessup's knight in shining armor.

14

Investigation Game

The twenty-four-hour mark had officially rolled around and Kelvin filed the missing person's report for Ivanka Renee` Jessup at exactly seven p.m. that night. The report was lengthy and described Ivy to a perfect T. Jesse had chosen a picture of his daughter, taken with her brother, Brenton, the day he had deployed to the Middle East. She looked beautiful and modest, just the way her father had always seen her. The apple of his eye in every fashion, Jesse had now grown extremely worried about what had happened to his daughter. Up to that point, it had never occurred to him that Antonio Rodriguez may have taken her and it was the furthest thing from his mind. He still held on to the notion that she may show up, after choosing to get a wild ass hair and do something completely out of her character. Reality was not something he wanted to face, but when Kelvin handed him the copy of the report, Jesse shivered in fear and realization that Ivy was, in fact, missing. He had hard copy evidence of that fact.

He stared at the form and shook his head. Everything was there in black and white. It all seemed too formal to him. So impersonal and regulated. There was no life to it. Just black words typed boldly into little bar fields. This was supposed to be the thing that helped him get his daughter home? Jesse could not fathom it. It was just a piece of paper with a lot of words. There was no power in it. There was no way to know anything about where Ivy was. He wondered what the purpose of the paper was, other than a trail to show the cops did something. It was not as if it took Kelvin forever to type it up and file it. Jesse thought the worst part was honestly on himself and his wife. The cops did not seem to honestly care, and he was starting to understand his wife's position on the matter. If he chose to act like Margie did, however, he knew he would land his ass in a firm jail cell in less than half an hour. He folded the page and stuck it in his back pocket as Kelvin began speaking to him.

"That will about do it for now, Jesse. All you need to do is start posting flyers, and we will ask around, see if we find out anything useful. If we do, we will get ahold of you as soon as possible," he explained.

Jesse stared back at him blankly. His explanation was not what he had expected and it gnawed on his conscience. "You mean that's it? There isn't anything else for us to do but wait? That seems like an awful lot of wasted time, energy, and office supplies, if you ask me," he stated, dumbfounded by the entire ordeal. Jesse shook his head and waved Kelvin off. "Don't worry about it, Officer Matthews, you just do your job and let a father handle figuring out the specifics. I guess I need to form my own party to find her. Mark my words, though, if something has happened to my daughter, and this department does not do everything, and I mean everything, in their power to help find out what is going on, I'm going to cause the biggest stink the town of Decaturville has ever seen. You can bet your bottom dollar on that, sir," he said, immediately exiting the building.

Kelvin exhaled a long, annoyed breath. Truth was Kelvin did care more than he let on, but he had rules to stick to. Rules he hated, most days, and felt prevented him from doing his civic duty to the best of his ability. He was only assistant captain, but Captain Buchanan ran a tight ship, and he was always by the book on everything. Every arrest and every traffic warning was done specifically to a set of perfect rules. Buchanan had it in his mind that a good department meant following all the rules by dotting every *i* and crossing every *t*. Sometimes, Kelvin thought he went overboard, and making him wait to get Ivy's case going was one of those instances. Buchanan was not from Decaturville, as Kelvin and the other officers on the force were. He had been hired by the town as a replacement captain, after they lost the previous captain to an unexpected heart attack. Instead of hiring one of the long-standing employees or officers for the job, the town chose to outsource the job on an employment site. It was a situation that infuriated the rest of the officers, and for reasons just like the one Kelvin was currently involved in, the majority of the cops did not like him.

Jesse crossed the street to where Aaron waited for him in the truck and shook his head as he plopped into the passenger side seat. "The report is filed, but I don't think it's going to do shit for us. They act like we are some kind of idiots a piece of paper can save. I mean, what kind of moron do they take me as? They're just going to sit on their butts, collecting dust and eating donuts in that office, while we do all the footwork. Shit, in the amount of time I have wasted waiting on Decaturville Police Department, I could have asked everybody in the damn town when the last time they saw Ivanka was. Damn, Margie was right," he muttered. Aaron's eyes widened and he gripped the steering wheel to anchor himself.

"I guess that means you want me to drive, Mr. Jessup?" he asked. The question was meant to be rhetorical and was met with a look that settled the argument without the need for Jesse's approval.

"How am I supposed to tell my wife all this?" Jesse stated in a low tone.

Aaron busied himself with the driving and kept his eyes on the road. Things were not going how he had imagined they would when he came to Decaturville for the job. Kelvin had not said it, but Aaron knew there was going to be a list of people who were considered the usual suspects in a missing person's case. With him being the newest person in town, it put him at the top of the list. Though he had not said anything about it, he was beginning to wonder if the police were going to use the usual methods and question everyone about Ivy. If that were the case, they would be losing time by coming to ask the Jessups or him about her. That made Jesse right on every account. Their discovery at the diner had come up empty, and it seemed to him, there was nothing else they could do on that end. The gears of Aaron's mind started turning as he started thinking out the possibility that someone in town had done something to Ivy. There was only one person who stuck out in his mind as he considered all the possible motives a person could have in taking Ivanka Jessup. The first name to pop into his mind was Antonio Rodriguez. Aaron turned to look at Jesse and squeezed the steering wheel. He was not sure if he should mention it or wait, but with time flying by and the uncertainty of what could be happening to Ivy, he let his thoughts slip out to become the next sentence.

"Jesse, you need to start thinking about who possible suspects for abduction could be. That being said, I recognize myself as being the new guy in town and that puts me at the top of the list, however, I think we need to consider who had something against you or Ivy. Who in town would have a reason to hurt her?" he said.

Jesse looked back at him with a glint in his eye. It dawned

on him in that instance that he had not been thinking of the possibility of someone with a vendetta against Ivy. Everyone loved his daughter, that he knew of. The list of suspects was beyond him, but as he steadied his gaze on Aaron, he started wondering.

"You are definitely onto something there, Aaron. Only people in town I can think of who may be mad at her or want to hurt her would be Bud or maybe..." His voice trailed off as they passed by the factory where Antonio worked. His Ford Ranger was parked close to the road, and Jesse tapped the dashboard with his finger as they passed it. "Wait a minute. Pull over and park the truck out of the way. I don't want anyone to spot it. You and I are about to do some Texan investigating our damn selves," he finished.

Aaron followed the instruction and pulled the truck over, in the shadow of a large evergreen tree. He turned to look at his boss and furrowed his eyebrow. "What is that, boss man?" he asked curiously.

Jesse nodded to the factory. It was a manufacturing plant that employed most of the workers in Decaturville. They made plastic housings for various companies. The stench of melted plastic filled the air for miles, and the place was known for hiring a lot of undocumented workers. Immigrants from Mexico and South America easily got jobs there, and most of them did not speak a single word of English. Jesse was by no means racist, and growing up in Southern Texas, he was used to the bicultural atmosphere, but something about that truck made his blood boil. There was one Mexican he could not stand, and it was the owner of that vehicle.

"See that truck over yonder." Jesse pointed out the Ranger.

Aaron followed his finger and recognized the vehicle in a matter of a few seconds. "Ah, that is the guy I punched's truck, right?" he asked. "Wasn't the name Antonio something or another?" he inquired.

Jesse nodded and eased the door open to step out onto the ground. "Sure is, and I want to go have a look-see at it," he stated. "Come on, Aaron, let's go check something out."

Aaron stepped out of the vehicle and followed after Jesse. They crossed the road and snuck into the parking lot, looking around closely to watch for any security guards or lot attendants.

Jesse approached the truck with suspicion and immediately began scanning the interior cab for anything out of the ordinary. There wasn't a single thing he noticed out of the way. His lips flat lined and he put his hands up in frustration, placing his palms against the side of his head.

"Let's have a look at the truck bed, boss man. Just 'cause you didn't find anything in the cab doesn't mean you won't find something in the back," Aaron reassured him. As he spoke, he strode around to the back and started looking inside. The bed was fairly empty, save for a few plastic bottles and a beer can or two. Nothing seemed to stick out, but as Aaron scanned, he noticed a piece of torn rope tied to a hook on the side of the truck bed. It was not anything unusual to see in someone's truck bed in Texas, but what stuck out was a single dark smear on the fibers. He waved Jesse over and pointed at the rope. "Do you see that, boss man?" he asked.

Jesse looked at the rope and gave a shrug. "It's a hogtie. These people tend to have outdoor hog barbecues a lot. Not an unusual thing to see," he stated.

Aaron quirked a brow. He was not so convinced that it was as innocent as Jesse believed it to be. "Yeah, I know what it is, but do you see the red stain on it? That looks like blood," he finished.

Jesse shook his head as if it did not matter.

Aaron could not understand how the man was not following his train of thought and narrowed his eyes in frustration. He may have thought it was human blood, or rather, *Ivy's blood*, but convincing anyone else that the rope was anything more than a hogtie as Jesse had stated was going to take work. As much as Aaron wanted to rip the rope out of the truck and burn rubber back to the police department with his evidence, he knew that would not bode well. He gave a sigh and finally the fire to his ass lit up.

"Why in the hell did you even have us get out of the damn truck to waltz over here and have a gander at this damn truck? We haven't found a damn lick of anything, and we sure as hell don't even know what to look for. Yeah, it's a hog tie. You're right. Let's get the hell out of here and go see your wife. I bet the woman needs some consoling, which, I might add, you have not done such a great job of giving her. No offense to you, and I love my job at Jessup Farm, but this has gotten to be too damn much for me. I came here for a ranch hand job not a vigilante investigator," he said, turning to walk back towards the vehicle. He shook his head, but the look of his face read as deep concern and upset. All Aaron wanted to do was find Ivy and tell her what he should have told her the night her mom caught wind of it—tell her that he would protect her, love her, and keep her safe at night. He had always wanted honey sunshine, and now, it seemed as if his chance had been torn away in the blinking of an eye.

Jesse stood dumbfounded. If it had been over anything else, he probably would have given Aaron a rebuking like the boy had not seen since adolescence, but something about the way Aaron said it, reminded him of his son, Brenton. His body language told him Aaron was having a hard time handling the stress of the situation and was starting to really get unnerved. Worry was written all over his face, and it occurred to Jesse that he cared more about Ivy than he had let on. Again, Margaret had been proven right. As he thought of her, he looked back at the rope one last time and gave a sigh. Aaron was right; this had been a stupid idea and an even stupider waste of time, when his wife was at the farm, waiting to hear back from him. He jogged after Aaron and sighed as he pulled himself back into the passenger seat.

Aaron had already cranked the truck and buckled himself in. He sat staring at the windshield with a look of distress painted across his features.

Jesse looked at him and exhaled deeply. "Aaron, you are right about everything you said out there. I have been real dumb, and I am wasting time when my wife needs me and my daughter is in danger. You have done a great job of being a supportive friend and a great employee. I owe you an apology for how I have been acting. Hope you can take it, 'cause I'm not known to be a man who easily swallows his pride," he stated.

Aaron looked at him and eased his foot onto the gas. He crept the truck onto the road and nodded. "Just because we didn't find anything conclusive doesn't mean we shouldn't keep an eye on old Antonio. I get the feeling something isn't right. Something odd is going on around here, and we just need to keep our eyes peeled. We need to get a party started. You know anybody with some good hunting dogs or blood hounds?" he asked.

Jesse had an epiphany, in that second. There were two bloodhounds, owned by a friend of his in the next town over, Haleton.

"Yeah, I got a friend who lives about fifteen miles away in Haleton; he owns two bloodhounds. He uses them mainly for company but they help him out on hunting trips, at times. He's a good buddy of mine; we go way back. He watched Ivy and Brenton grow up, and his kids were close friends of theirs. Actually, it was his son who Brent went into the Army with. I know he will be willing to help, if I explain the situation. Let's get back to the house so I can give him a call and let him know what is going on. I think if we get Duke and Lady out to the diner, we may have a trail in no time. Faster than Kelvin Matthews is working, anyway," he said.

It was the first good news Aaron had heard all day. The bloodhounds would give them a step in the right direction, and he gave a half smile.

"Don't worry, Mr. Jessup. We will find out what happened to Ivy. One way or another," he said.

15

There Ain't Nothing Like a
Hound Dog

A ntonio pulled up to the junkyard after work and snorted as he walked towards the office. He gave the grease monkey inside a glance over and murmured in heavily accented English, "I got that girl. How much you going to pay me for your go at it? And I want my coca. I have some clients who are out. When is my shipment supposed to get here?" he asked.

The man sitting at the desk glared at him. "Listen here, Tonio, I have the meth cooking in the back, the pot coming in tomorrow, and the coca will be here in two days. I suggest you check the fuckin' attitude. If you got the girl, I want you to bring her here so I can sell her to the cartel, when they come in two days. She better be in as good shape as you said she looked or I'm not going to sell you anymore for vending," the man said. It was the same man who Aaron and Jesse had asked about the transmission for the Datsun, Jon Littleton. He was a despicable character with no morals and deep roots in the drug scene. He supplied the area with marijuana, cocaine, methamphetamines, and pills. The junkyard was a front business to keep the authorities off his back. Given his tendency to use people like Antonio to do his running, he had continuously gotten away with his trade for years. The sale of young girls in the area was something he did on rare occasions, but Antonio had promised this blonde beauty would collect a fine ransom. The price, however, was going to cost him dealing with Antonio's stupidity and cockiness. A combination Jon had little tolerance for.

"That is some bullshit, Jon. I do so much. Ju treat me like shit, man," Antonio said in a huff. His eyes were brimmed red, and Jon could sense he had not slept much in the past few hours.

"Well, deal with it, or your ass won't get any of the shipment. When can you bring me the girl?" he asked.

Antonio did not really want to get rid of Ivy, just yet. He had been having far too much fun with the girl to just pass her off to the next in line that quickly. He knew, however, that Rosalia had seen her, and that was unsettling for him. Every moment he spent away, he worried if Rosalia would do something foolish and try helping the girl. His sister's religious tendencies were a nuisance, but she had gotten them from his deceased mother. It was the only reminder Antonio had of anything good in his life. Without Rosalia, Antonio would have gone off the deep end a lot sooner and more victims would have paid the price. Rosalia was the calming water who kept Antonio at bay.

"I will bring her to ju tomorrow night. I can't come back here tonight," he said.

Jon nodded and pulled an envelope out of a drawer, passing it to Antonio. "This is your money for delivering the girl in one piece, by tomorrow night. I expect you to bring her or else I'm going to have my amigos give you a visit. I don't think you want to have them come by and get a hold on Rosie, do you?" he said with a grin.

Antonio tore the envelope open to find two grand stuffed

inside. The amount he had agreed to be paid for taking the girl from her job. He grinned and stuffed it into the front of his pocket. "I will bring her, and ju won't touch Rosalia," he said, walking away.

Jon grinned and planted his feet back on the desk. Antonio was sadistic and cruel, but Jon Littleton was the brain of the operation, a demented individual without a single ounce of caring anywhere in his body. The door slammed and Jon whirled his swivel chair around to peer at the calendar.

"That old bastard thinks he is smart. We will see. Yeah, buddy, we will see," he retorted.

Antonio pulled up to Bud's Motorbike Bar at exactly eight fifteen. He parked his truck and strode inside, where Luis was already sitting in their usual booth.

"Oye, vato." Luis waved him over. There were two beers sitting on the table, and Antonio grabbed the second as he took a seat. "Hey, chingow, that was my extra one!" Luis exclaimed.

Antonio pulled the bottle to his lips and took a long chug. He looked back at Luis and replaced the beer on the table with a smug expression. "Not anymore, ese. What ju was doing? Ju didn't go to work today, but here ju are, lazy ass drinking cerveza like nothing," he said.

Luis gave a nod and took a drink out of his first beer. "I got sick this morning. I don't think we should hab taken dat girl, Antonio," he said. "I think we made a bad mistake and ju should let her go now."

Antonio looked back at him and scoffed. "Ju are serious, man? Ju know what is going to happen if I let her go, don't ju? She is going to go straight to the policia, and I am going to la carcel again."

Luis gave a knowing glance and took another swing of beer. "Ju think I don't know that, Tonio? Ju think I have not been thinking about this all day? I could not go to work, acting like eberythang is okay. Eberythang is not okay, Tonio. How ju would feel if somebody stole Rosalia? I been thinking how I would feel if somebody took off with my Santa, and I don't like this. It just does not feel right. Mi madrecita would beat me for doing something like this. Y las drogas. I don't like the guy we are working with. That guey does not seem fair to me. Something is not right," Luis explained.

Antonio could not believe what he was hearing, and it was not good, considering his involvement with the kidnapping. Luis knew too much, and if he decided to go saint on him, asking forgiveness for his sins, he could turn on Tonio and Jon any second. Antonio chugged the rest of his beer, and stood up. "I think ju been thinking too much, Luis. Drink some more cerveza and chill out. Ju mind is just feeling the lack of alcohol." He laughed as he stated it.

Luis rolled his eyes, and finished off his beer. His hand slid to his pocket and he extracted his cellphone to look down at the time. He could always do what was right and go to the cops. He had considered it several times, but he feared the repercussions against his wife, Santa, and daughter, Isabela. He replaced the phone and looked back up to see Antonio walking over with two more beers.

"Here ju go, amigo. Dos cervezas, and lots of time to enjoy them, eh?" he smirked.

Luis gave a nod.

"Si, Tonio. If ju say so. My stomach is not feeling so good. I think I should go home to Santa and Isa early, tonight. I need to work tomorrow. I called out today, but now mi cheque is going to be small," he stated.

Antonio shook his head in disagreement. "Oh, ju don't worry about the fabrica cheque. Chingala, we are going to make a lot of money on this next deal with El Jefe. I'm telling ju, this time is going to be real good." Tonio pulled out the envelope with the money and placed it on the table. "Ju ready for ju cut, amigo? How does mil dolares sound?" He winked.

Luis looked down at the envelope and gulped. His hand slid forward and he opened it to find the two grand Jon had paid for the secure arrival of the girl, Ivy Jessup.

"What is this for, Tonio?" he asked.

"What do ju mean? Is for la puta, Ibanka. I told ju I was going to take good care of her, remember?" He laughed.

Luis shook his head. "This is blood money, Tonio. I don't want anything like that. I tell ju this eberytime, and ju neber listen. Why ju put me in these positions, eh?" he asked.

Tonio groaned and rolled his eyes. "What the fuck, Luis? What crawled up jur ass and made ju un Santo? Ju think ju are something special? Ju grabbed her first, ese, or did ju forget that already?" he asked.

Luis shuddered. While it was true that he had helped kidnap Ivanka and had been the one who knocked her out and tied her up, he had never considered selling her into the Mexican sex slave industry. American girls did bring a pretty price, but Luis had never been into the prostitution part of the business. When Antonio introduced him to Jon, he had only been interested in making some extra money to send back to the rest of his family in Mexico. His only interest was in selling marijuana. He had never wanted to get into the cocaine, meth, or pills. On the street, Luis only did the pot deals, and that was what he always wanted to do. It was not until the past few months, Tonio had gotten into selling the coke, and the money was addictive to him. He squandered it right and left, while Luis sent it back home every Friday. Luis had considered leaving Texas and taking what little he had left with him. He knew he could leave an anonymous tip about where Ivy was, but time was running short. His reason for meeting Antonio at the bar that night was to try to talk some sense into him about not selling the girl. It was obvious that Tonio had already received payment for the product delivery, Ivanka, and that was something Luis had not prepared for.

"This is wrong, Tonio! I told ju when we started, I was not going to hurt people. This was to make extra money. This is fucked up. Ju got paid to deliver somebody's hija to los maranos de Tijuana." He glared angrily at him. Luis shook his head and took one last drink of his beer. "I don't want this chingalera. Ju keep jur money, Tonio. I am not getting involved. I hab my daughter and wife to think of. Ju are in deep shit now, ju know that? Ay, Dios mio," he said, walking away.

Tonio's mouth fell open and he flipped Luis the bird as he walked off. "Pinche idiota. Ju think ju are some kind of saint. Ju think that Jesus is going to rescue ju in the middle of the night, and the unicorns is going to come in like the calvary," he muttered under his breath. There was a new bartender working the counter and she caught Antonio's eye as he looked back over at her. She was a little older than Ivanka but had all the right curves in all the right places. "Mamacita," Antonio called, waving her towards him. The bartender tilted her head and came out from behind the counter.

"Everything okay here? You need another drink, sir?" she asked with a dazzling smile.

Antonio grinned from ear to ear and gave a nod. "Everything is perfect, mamacita. Ju think ju can bring me two shots of Patron? La cerveza is good but I think, tonight, I need something a liddo stronger. Ju know?" he asked.

The bartender, Stacy, gave a nod. "Sure thing, I'll bring you a double shot of Patron in just a second." She waltzed away, giving Antonio a great shot of her rounded backside. Tonio admired it with a click of the tongue and a nod. "Yes, mami, ju will." He grinned.

"Here you are," Stacy said. She placed the drink on the table and walked away again.

Antonio slammed the shot down quickly and shook his head. "Ah, que rico." He smiled.

Jesse and Aaron had been home for a while, and in that time, Jesse had managed to get seven people interested in helping him search for Ivy. The owner of the bloodhounds was William Hearle. He and his wife, Wendy, were two of the people willing to go look for Ivy. Along with them, he had gotten the pastor from his church, his wife, the neighbor and his wife, and the ranch hand who helped them. The party was made up of the Hearles, Jessups, Aaron, Pastor James Linn and Mary Linn, Suzanne and Bobby Mitchell, and Scott Windsor, their ranch hand. That made it a complete party of ten people and two dogs, Duke and Lady. It was Jesse's hope that, with that many people, they could cover more ground and ask more townsfolk if they had seen or heard anything out of the ordinary. They decided to get a start on the searching at daylight.

"Well, it looks like we should get to bed, Jesse," Margie said, looking at the clock on the wall.

"Yeah, I reckon so. Hey, Aaron, you want to sleep here on the couch tonight, instead of hauling back to the barn apartment? Feel free to sit here and watch TV. Whatever you want," Jesse said as he walked towards his bedroom.

"Thanks, Mr. Jessup, I think I will do just that," Aaron said.

Margie pulled a quilt off the back of her chair and tossed it over to Aaron.

"Keep yourself warm, kid," she said with a smile.

Just as she began to saunter away, Aaron piped up, "Mrs. Jessup, err, Margie, you mind if I ask you a question?"

"Sure, Aaron, what is it?" she said, leaning against the wall and crossing her arms.

"You asked me the other day what kind of girl I wanted and then you mentioned a honey sunshine. Was there something you were hinting at?" he inquired.

"Oh, well, I guess by this point it is okay to tell you." She sighed, "I know my daughter rather well, you know. I could tell Ivanka liked you, and if I were wholly honest, I think you like her, too," she said.

"Oh," he replied. "Yeah, I thought it may have been something like that, when Ivy told me her nickname. I..." He paused in contemplation before continuing, "I do like her, and I am really starting to feel sick, worrying about her. I was not able to tell you all about what happened this afternoon. With me and Jesse, I mean," he said.

"What do you mean, Aaron? What else happened?" she asked.

Aaron went into detail about the factory and the investigation he and Jesse had embarked on. "The thing is I saw something that stood out to me, but it did not to Jesse," Aaron said.

"What was it, Aaron?" Margie asked him, puzzled.

"A rope with dried blood on it. It was in the back of Antonio's truck, but Jesse said it was a hog tie," he stated.

"A hog tie? Hmm, I think you may be on to something, Aaron. We need to let the dogs near Antonio's truck and that rope," she stated.

Aaron gave a nod and lay back down against the couch. "I thought so, too, and I really think there is something not right about how quickly our incident with him took place, in correlation with Ivanka's disappearance. I just hope the hounds are able to do more than we have," he said.

Margie smiled and started off down the hallway. "Sleep well, Aaron, and know I am really thankful for all you have done—all you keep doing for our family. It is above and beyond what anyone could expect from their hired hand," she murmured.

Aaron peered up at the ceiling and exhaled deeply. "Ivy, wherever you are, I promise you I am going to find you, and when I find out who hurt you, I am going to fuck up their world. I promise," he said. In moments, Aaron drifted off to sleep, with Ivanka's face being the last thing on his mind.

16

Fraying Edges

Antonio sauntered into his bedroom well past three o'clock in the morning. Ivy had since been given water and food several times. Rosalia even took it upon herself to read Ivy some of the Bible. The difference between Antonio and his sister was like night and day. For as dark as his soul was, Rosalia was the complete opposite. She was caring, considerate, grateful, and compassionate. Everything a young lady should be at her age. Ivy enjoyed talking to her, and with every hour they spent together, Rosalia gave her hope she could be free. She had chosen to read Exodus and the way Moses led the Israelites out of Egypt—how they had spent forty years in the desert and all they had gone through. It gave Ivy a glimmer of belief that maybe God had heard the prayers she had made to him while Antonio had raped and beaten her. Though, as of yet, no prayer had been answered and her tormentor's voice filtered into her ears as she awoke.

"Good morning, Ibanka, ju ready for some more fun?" Antonio asked. His breath smelled awful, of beer or liquor. Once again, Ivy was chilled when he tore the blanket from her naked body. "I am sure ready for some more of ju. Oh, yes. Ju so sweet and so ripe for the taking." He grinned.

In the darkness, she could barely see the glint of the moonlight across his teeth.

Instantly, he lowered himself down on top of her and rubbed his grimy palm down her stomach. "So beautiful, mamacita. Blanka and hermosa. Like a chicken." He chuckled wickedly at the joke. "Yes, just like a chicken. Tasty white meat that starts out pink. Then ju work it a little and it falls apart in ju mouth. Sweet taquitos ju chickens make." He roared with laughter.

Ivy held perfectly still, attempting to keep her breathing normal as Antonio's palms continued down her skin. She closed her eyes and inhaled a breath, enduring the touches. It was all she could do not to vomit in her mouth but she focused on the first good thing that entered her mind. In the moments when something terrible was happening, a person could find solace in his or her own head and what Ivy found there was the handsome chiseled face of Aaron Kilpatrick. She now wished she had followed her mother's advice and told him she was interested in learning more about him, in the possibility of a relationship, if one could be had.

Antonio took notice of Ivy's bodily movements and how she was not fighting as much as she had the first night. Though he was inebriated, he somehow managed to see she was more agreeable. "Oh, ju want to be a good girl now? Ju want to have my hands on ju now. I always knew ju would eventually come around, Ibanka. Ju could have been nice but ju had to get jur boyfriend to punch me. Ju had to be a bitch, and now, ju will be treated like a bitch," he said.

Ivy inhaled deeply and mumbled against the gag.

"What did ju say, Ibanka? Ju know I cannot hear ju with that stuff in jur mouth," he said. He pulled the gag from her lips and commanded her to speak, "Say it again, Ibanka. What ju need to tell me now?"

Ivy groaned and exhaled. "I am sorry I was so mean to you, Antonio. I treated you very badly. I should have been nicer to my customers. I should have given you a chance. I am sorry my father's employee hit you. He is not my boyfriend. I don't have a boyfriend but you can be him. You were right. I deserved this," she muttered. Her face fell into a sad expression and she hoped her acting skills were as polished as she had rehearsed in her head. From the look on Antonio's face, he believed it and he smiled from ear to ear.

"I told you that you would come around, Ibanka. The problem is it is too late for me to change my plans. I wish ju had listened before. I wish ju had done what I needed ju to do. Now, ju will have to go but we can have some more fun first. Ju liked what I did to ju, eh?" Antonio grinned.

Ivy gulped and gave a nod. It was all she could do not to curse him like the bastard dog he was, but she was still bound.

"Everything you did was what I needed, Antonio. You did what I needed, and I should be grateful. Let me show you how appreciative I can be," she said sweetly.

"How are ju going to do that?" Antonio asked.

"Oh, I have a bad imagination, Antonio. I can do such great things with my dirty little mouth," she stated.

Ivy's acting like the pretty little whore easily convinced Antonio so well. He gave a nod and pulled his bowie knife out. "Ju show me this then, but do not try to pull anything. I have two big dogs here, and they will maul ju to death if ju go out of this room," he said.

She acknowledged it and filed it in the back of her mind. It was valuable information for what she had hoped to do next.

Antonio cut the binds at her wrists but left the ankles tied.

"Okay, mami, what are ju going to do for me now?" he asked curiously.

Ivy smiled and leaned forward to press her lips against his. She trailed her fingers down his chest and toyed with his pecs through his shirt.

"Oh, do not worry, Papi. I will show you how much fun we will have for this last night, but you do not trust me enough to completely untie me. I cannot do what I want to do if I am still bound," she said with a pout.

Antonio groaned and looked back at the binds on her ankles. Due to being intoxicated, his mind did not register that Ivy was playing a game with him—a game he was falling for surprisingly easily. He shook his head suddenly and pulled her back against him. "No, ju let me touch ju like this for a little bit. I want ju to keep facing me. I want to taste jur sweet lips on mine."

His palms pressed against her cheeks and pulled her back to kiss him. The stench of liquor permeated the air and the vapors seemed to fill Ivy's mouth as he snuck his tongue between her lips. Ivy was beginning to feel green around the gills but she kissed him back, again trailing her fingers down his chest and towards his belt buckle.

"That's it, Mami. Keep that up, right there. Ju just do not stop. Mmm," he said against her lips.

Ivy did as he bid and her fingers began to unbuckle the belt. Using womanly wiles against him was really starting to look like it might work but she worried about the dogs he had mentioned or what else may lay in wait on the opposing side of the door. Her only hope was that she could persuade Antonio to untie her ankles and fall asleep with her. She prayed it would work, and if sleeping with Antonio as a willing victim was needed, it was a risk she had prepared to take. She broke away from the kiss and began laying caresses across his throat. She continued down over his collarbone and furiously started unbuttoning his shirt.

Antonio smiled and slid his fingers into her hair. The tips of his nails clawed into her scalp and Ivy did her best not to cry out in pain. Antonio was enjoying it so much that a deep moan escaped his throat. Ivy shuddered but continued with the kissing. Further and further still, until she reached the top of his unfastened belt. It was now or never and providing the service she had thought of was the only thing she could think would distract him long enough for her to ease the bowie knife from his pants.

Ivy focused on Aaron as she continued to perform the deed. This was not something she had ever done before but it seemed to be working. She figured all the smut novels she had read in her life must have given her a good education and continued to perform just as she had been.

"Oh, ju are too good, mamacita. Dame un beso," he said, claiming her lips in a deep kiss. Ivy struggled to breathe as her hand continued to stroke and coax him further into her trap.

She now regretted the offer she had made. What she had hoped would happen was not what Antonio had in mind. Antonio held her head still against the pillow as Ivy stared up at him with horror and pain filled eyes.

Suddenly, Antonio seized up and began convulsing as he moaned loudly into the night, "Ay, si, ay. Mm, mami."

Ivy struggled to breathe and closed her eyes in terror. It was a nightmare exchange, and all she wanted now was to get as far as she could from this monster and find a way to her family. After a few seconds, she finally found the strength to speak. "Can I please have some water?" she asked in a hoarse voice.

Antonio glanced over at the pitcher from earlier and shrugged. "I guess ju can," he said. The glass remained just out of reach and Antonio leaned forward to grab it and hand to her.

Ivy took it and gulped it down quickly. Antonio watched her closely and sighed.

"Thank you," she finally said, handing the glass back.

Antonio gave a nod and replaced it on the table. He then fell back onto the bed and sighed pleasantly. "Now, I will go to sleep. Ju can stay untied. Ju are not going nowhere with the dogs out there," he murmured. So certain that everything was going his way, Antonio had begun to grow complacent, just as Ivanka hoped he would. The knife remained in his pants pocket, and Antonio completely forgot about it as he fell asleep beside her.

Ivy breathed a sigh of relief, but her heart still beat wildly in her chest from the cock sucking and face fucking she had endured. While her planning had worked to a degree, she still had no clothes and it was cold outside. This was something she knew would prove to be a challenge and going out the front door was not completely out of the question. The small window was the only hope she had of escaping her prison and the torment Antonio had forced her to endure. She sighed and stilled herself against the bed as she considered what the best escape route would be. Luckily, Rosalia had left the poncho on the ground and she could use it as a covering. If she could just find a neighbor or a car passing by on the road, she could get the help needed to get out of this place. It was not yet the time to try to escape, however, and she lay there, thinking about what to do next. She only had a few hours to make an effort to free herself. Only a few options had presented, and she needed to make absolute certain this was flawless, if she wanted to survive.

Hours later, Ivy awoke to find herself pinned beneath Antonio's arm. Silently, she cursed at her unfortunate luck. How was she going to get out of this situation? With her ankles still bound to the footboard, she had no idea how she would get out of the bed. The small bowie knife he had used to cut the binds was in the pocket furthest from her and getting it was going to be no small feat. She eased his arm from her body and prayed he would not wake up, as she thought out her plan of action.

Antonio rolled to his side as she pushed his arm off. Ivy held her breath, in fear he would awaken, and watched as he eased himself into the position. In seconds, the sounds of his snoring filled the room and Ivy sighed in relief. The pocket in which the bowie knife resided was now visible, and she leaned forward to ease her index and thumb inside, reaching in to grab for the blade. Her fingers brushed against it, and gently, she began inching it out of his pocket. Each centimeter she pulled it out seemed like an eternity, and though she was closer to having it free now than she had been before, Ivy felt as if extracting it fully would never happen. Closer and closer, she pulled it towards herself until, finally, it slid from his pocket. She gripped it tightly and pulled the sheathing from it. She sat up abruptly and slid the blade down between her right ankle and the rope binding. Gently, she began to cut the rope until it finally frayed to release her ankle. With a sigh and a grin, Ivy slid her leg to drape over the bed's edge as she began to work on the last bind that kept her bound to the footboard. In moments, she was free, but this was only the beginning.

Ivy still needed to get the poncho, which was a foot away from her on the ground. Slowly, she slid her body from the bed to land in a crouch on the floor. She peered up at Antonio as he slept and leaned forward to crawl towards the covering. As her fingers neared it, Ivy feared the floorboards would creak but it was a risk she had to take. She now had the poncho, and rising to a stand, she pulled it down over her head. The next task would be crossing the floor to the window that was at least a foot higher than she reached. She would have to pull herself to lift her body up and climb outside. There was no possible way to move something to stand on, without waking the sleeping giant. Ivy inhaled and held her breath as she tiptoed across the floor. Her eyes never left Antonio as she made her way towards the window. The poncho scarcely covered her battered body and braving the elements as she was would be another hurdle in and of itself.

She had no time to think about the possibilities, and being that she had no idea where she was, she had no idea what sort of animal life was around her. If she had been able to stay alert when Luis and Antonio had kidnapped her, the possibility of recognizing landmarks would have made her realize she was twenty miles away from Decaturville, on a country road in Haleton. The closest house was three miles away from Antonio's home but Ivy had no clue of this. It was now or never. The moment of truth had finally arrived and freedom was so close. Ivy had reached the sill of the window and noticed that it still remained cracked open about a half an inch. She eased the tips of her fingers beneath the sill and gently pushed it upward. The window creaked slightly and she squirmed in fear. Instantly, her eyes flashed back to Antonio, but he was completely dead to the world. Ivy shuddered and looked back at the window. She urged it up a bit more until it was a third of the way open. This was just enough space for her to crawl through. Now, the really difficult task came. She still had the knife and she dropped it out the window, quickly hearing it thud on the ground, seconds later. It was a five-foot drop from sill to the ground, but she had no choice. She pulled herself up to the window and eased her feet outside. With a final glance at Antonio's sleeping body, Ivy dropped herself to the ground and landed in a crouch.

It was pitch black and Ivy had no clue which way to go. Her eyes flashed from side to side as her fingers searched for the knife. Finally, she found it and gripped it in her hand. She stood up and looked back at the house, finding she was in the backyard. This gave her enough information to know to cross to the front and she immediately began running in that direction. As she came out into the front yard, she noticed a long gravel road that was barely illuminated beneath the moonlight. The nearest street lamp was an old wooden one that hardly gave off enough light to make the highway recognizable. She began to jog towards it. The gravel bit into her feet and tore into her skin but Ivy continued to run. Faster and faster down the drive, hoping she would reach the road quickly. The poncho fluttered to and fro as she ran, brushing across her kneecaps and giving the air time to caress her bared skin beneath it with every hurried step. Ivy had escaped Antonio's house but she still had not escaped his land. Would she ever get back home now? Ivy did not know, but the closer she came to the road, the more she gained the hope her family would find her. One way or another, Ivanka Jessup was going to survive and that was the only objective on her mind.

"You will make it, Ivy. You will just keep going," she whispered to herself.

17

The Search Begins

Aaron had trouble sleeping for most of the night, and by the time Jesse came in to wake him for the search, he was way past ready to go.

"Are we supposed to meet the rest of them somewhere specific?" Aaron asked as he stood up from the couch.

"Faraway Diner, since that was the place Ivanka went missing from. We are going to bring one of her dirty shirts from the laundry so the dogs can get a good sniffing of her scent," Jesse said.

Margie emerged from her room, dressed and ready to go. "Let's get a move on, boys. I want to get as many hours in looking for her as we can today," she said, walking past them. She paused at the door and looked back at Jesse as she directed her speech towards Aaron. "I want to get that rope you talked about from Antonio's truck and let the dogs get a whiff of it. I'm going to take my own car and I want you to ride with me, Aaron. Jesse can get the ranch hand from the neighbor to help him out," she stated firmly.

Jesse looked back at his wife and shook his head. "You'd better be careful, Margie. Just because we have had beef with

Antonio Rodriguez in the past, does not mean he did something with Ivy. You snoop too much and you may get yourself into trouble. You had better not go off halfcocked like you did at the police station. You know you eased yourself out of there with luck that Kelvin didn't lock you up for your actions downtown," he murmured, walking out the door past her.

Margie rolled her eyes and motioned to Aaron. "Come on, Kilpatrick. Let's go find out what the deal is with old Antonio. I have a notion you are onto something, and I want to follow that lead.

Aaron nodded, deciding it was best not to get caught up in the middle of Margaret and Jesse's disagreement. Beneath the surface, he could tell Margie loved Jesse and that he returned the sentiment. It was obvious to him, however, that Ivanka played mediator between the two of them a lot, and without her presence, they were getting along about like cats and dogs who are forced to live in the same house.

Jesse got into the truck, while Aaron and Margie got into Aaron's Camaro. Jesse gave a passing glance at his wife as he reversed and went on ahead of them. In a convoy, Aaron followed Jesse down the driveway and out onto the road. The rest of the way into town, they rode in silence. Margie watched out the window, and Aaron kept his gaze focused on driving. It seemed like an awkward situation, but the truth was Aaron figured Margaret needed time to think and reflect on the reality that she may have lost her daughter for good. Fact was after so many hours of someone being gone, the likelihood of them living through the ordeal was slim to none. Little did they know, Ivanka was braving the wilderness, less than fifteen miles from their farm. The only thing they could hope for was in believing in the majestic creature known to be most loyal to man, the canine.

Jesse pulled up to the diner first and slammed his truck door as he took lean against the vehicle. He had a look of disappointment spread out across his face, and he folded his arms as the Hearles pulled up in their Chevy. The blood-hounds were tied up in the back, and William and Wendy exited the cab with concerned looks on their faces.

"Morning, Jesse," William said.

"Good morning, Jesse. Where is Margie?" Wendy asked. Jesse nodded to the Camaro as Aaron and Margie parked.

"Right there." He nodded. Wendy acknowledged the vehicle just as Aaron and Margie stepped out to meet with them.

"Good morning, Willy, Wendy," Margie stated as she approached her husband and the group.

Wendy smiled and looked at Aaron inquisitively.

"This is Aaron Kilpatrick; he's our new ranch hand," Jesse said quickly.

William nodded and extended his hand. "Wish we could have met under better conditions, Aaron. I've heard a lot of good about you. Thank you for taking care of Jesse and Margie, here, for us. It's greatly appreciated," William said. He had a firm grip and Aaron gave a half smile.

"I agree. Nice to meet you, William, and you, Mrs. Hear-le," he said, releasing the grip on William's hand and offering to shake Wendy's.

"Likewise, Aaron," Wendy replied, shaking his hand quickly.

"Well, all right, did you bring Ivy's shirt or something Duke and Lady can get a good whiff of?" William asked.

Margie nodded and held out a white tank top. "She wore that the day before she went missing. It should have the freshest scent and it has not been washed yet," she said.

William took it and walked to the back of the truck. He held it out to Duke, first, and waited for the dog to give a loud snort. This was his cue that Duke had gotten enough scent to recognize the owner. Lady did the same thing and William smiled.

"So, here is how things will go. I am going to ride with Jesse, and Duke will come along with me. You and Aaron can ride with Wendy, and she will handle Lady. I guess we have a few more people to meet up with, right?" William said.

"Yes, we do, they should all be here shortly," Jesse said.

"Sounds good. So, we just wait it out, and when you are all ready, we will get things going," William stated.

Jesse inclined his head at William and stepped over to his wife's side. "You all right with that arrangement since you wanted to head out with Aaron on your own mission?" he asked.

She gave a nod and smiled. "That will be just fine and dandy, Mr. Jessup," she muttered. It was obvious Margie was still upset with Jesse, and her reason was because he had omitted the information about the rope. She walked towards Wendy with her arms folded, and Aaron gave Jesse a knowing glance. He had not meant to cause her to get mad at her husband, but he needed to talk to someone about what he had seen. Jesse had brought the consequences onto himself.

Pastor James Linn and his wife pulled up in a small Dodge pickup and stepped out. As if in unison, Bobby and Suzanne Mitchell pulled into the space beside them with their ranch hand, Scott Windsor, in their backseat. The Mitchells had a preference for driving their Subaru and that was the vehicle they stepped out of.

"Morning, Margie, Jesse. How you doing, Willy, Wendy?" Bobby asked as he walked towards the group. His wife and Scott were close on his heels as they closed the circle.

"Just waiting on you and getting the plan out," Jesse said. Everyone made their greetings and properly introduced himself or herself to Aaron. Enough time had passed to get the plan of action together and everyone was given stations and responsibilities. Aaron, Wendy, and Margie piled into the Chevy, and William and Jesse got into the Jessup's old beat up Ford. Scott was given the task of asking all the people at the diner who were regulars if they had seen or heard anything of the night of Ivy's disappearance. Bobby and Suzanne decided to go through a list of Ivy's old school friends and stake out her old job at Bud's, as well as ask the grocery store workers if Ivanka had been seen around there. Everyone had been given a stack of flyers with Ivanka's pictures and information on who to contact, if she was found. They decided they would post them all around Decaturville and Haleton. The next step was to post all her details on social media—Facebook and any other website they could think of, before they contacted the news with the story of Ivy's disappearance. It was the best plan they could all come up with, and they hoped that starting out at five o'clock in the morning, they could meet back at six o'clock that night with something to hand the police. As adamant as Jesse had been about Margie not going to snoop in Antonio's truck, Wendy Hearle was not in agreement. She thought Margie had a point, and when Aaron explained what he had seen, she got a womanly sense of intuition that something was a bit off about the whole situation and decided the first place she wanted to look was the truck bed. With Lady on her leash, she would sniff out the scent of Ivanka before they ever reached the truck, and if the rope held her DNA, there was no way the bloodhound would miss it.

"You know, Margie, if Lady sniffs out that blood, it may not be the kind of news you want to hear. Are you prepared to handle that, honey?" Wendy asked as she drove towards the factory.

Margie's voice broke as she looked at Wendy. "I honestly don't know, Wendy. I just don't know. I have not been thinking the worst, this whole time. I've been doing all I can to try to stay focused, except when it comes to Jesse. It just downright infuriates me that he did not have the decency to tell me what Aaron saw. It has been all I can do not to cry and cry. Hell, I don't even want to eat or cook. Just seems like my whole damn life is falling to pieces. I'm so heartbroken, and instead of my husband being supportive, he keeps reprimanding me like I am his daughter or something." She sobbed into her hands.

It made Aaron uncomfortable to be seated in the cab with the two women during an emotional and confident moment. He could sense that Wendy and Margaret had a years' long relationship, and whatever Margie held inside around everyone else, she wasn't afraid to let out to Wendy Hearle.

"Now, Margie, you know Jesse is a damn dumb ass mule most the time. I have been telling you that for over twenty years, but what you also know is the man loves you. He has been a great man and father to your babies. Men just don't show they care like women do," Wendy stated.

Margie nodded as Wendy looked back at the road. What the day held, nobody knew, but what was certain was they were trying to find Ivanka, one way or another.

Five o'clock in the morning came quickly, and Antonio awoke when Rosalia knocked on the door to tell him to get up for work.

"Hermano, it's time for you to get up," she said through the door.

Antonio's eyes cracked open, and he turned to look at the side Ivy was supposed to be on. Immediately, he sat up and started screaming obscenities and accusations at Rosalia.

"Chingada madre, Rosalia! Get in here!" he roared.

Rosalia opened the door and put her head inside the doorway.

"What's wrong, Hermano?" she asked. It didn't take long for her to realize what was wrong and her eyes widened as she began shaking her head. "No, no, I didn't do anything. I didn't do anything but give her water and food. I promise. I promise!"

"Where the hell is Ibanka then, Rosalia?" Antonio seethed.

Rosalia turned and ran from the bedroom, heading straight for the front door in a frantic, and fearful attempt to flee. There was nothing she could say to convince her brother she was innocent, and the fourteen-year-old's natural instinct was to get as far away from him as possible. How Ivanka had escaped, Rosalia didn't know, but she was secretly thankful the girl had gotten away. Now she considered how she would get away and if there was any way to find someone to take her in. Rosalia's parents had died when she was eleven, and she had lived with Antonio since. She had suffered his sadistic violent behaviors and constant drinking for years, but in realization that Ivanka was free, Rosalia began jogging down that same driveway Ivy had fled down with only one thought on her mind—to get help.

Ivy was in the midst of a thicket in the woods and had been working her way through it for the past thirty minutes. As soon as she had made it out to the road, the reality of open space made her realize finding cover was important so she could keep hidden, in the event Antonio awoke to find her gone. It had been two hours since she had escaped, but she still had not come to the next house. Her arrival would have come much sooner, if she had stuck to the road, but the risk was just too high. The fear of being caught and taken back to endure the torture Antonio had given her was just too paralyzing. Her feet bled from cuts and scrapes, and her body was riddled with bruises from head to toe. Even with all her pains, Ivy forced herself forward and each step she made in the forest was counted as a step towards home. It was still very cold and the sun had barely come over the horizon to cast ribbons of golden light across the landscape. The trees appeared skeletal but they helped in keeping her body shadowed from sight.

She had not stopped once, since beginning her voyage, but thirst was beginning to weaken her body to the point of extreme exhaustion. The need for water was imminent, and Ivy knew it. As she continued further into the woods, she hoped to come across a brook or creek to drink from. The benefits of learning how to survive on Texan land were something she now had a great deal of appreciation for. Ivy knelt down, suddenly, and lowered her head. "Dear God, please just let me find some help soon." She was damn near freezing and the poncho was doing a poor job of keeping her warm. Ivy continued to pray softly, "Please bring the sun higher so I can get a moment's rest from this," she said. A tear welled in her right eye and slid down her cheek.

Ivy stood again and pushed a branch out of her way as she strode further into the forest. Her feet snapped a twig and she cursed as a thorn embedded deeply into her foot, "Son-of-a-bitch." She didn't know how much more she could take. If it were not for the strength she had mustered in her will to survive, Ivy would have passed out in the first thirty minutes. If she had been able to see herself, she would have been afraid her face was completely shattered and needed reconstructive surgery. Her right eye was completely swollen and her lip had split in three different directions. There was a gash on her left arm and the back of her head had a huge knot from all the slapping and rough handling Antonio had given her. She did not look anything like she normally did, and it was highly likely, nobody would recognize her. After a few more steps, she finally came to the edge of a small ditch. There was a slow-moving stream that flowed through it and just enough water for her to catch some in her palm. Ivy leapt at the opportunity and dove down to lay on her stomach. Sprawled out on the forest floor, she scooped up a drink and continued to cup it into her mouth. She did this several times in succession, until water had covered her drying lips and rolled down her chin. She then cupped some more and lifted it to her face. It was freezing and stung as it met with each cut on her skin, but Ivy was thankful. After she had consumed enough, Ivy stood up again, and feeling a bit more revitalized, she began to jog the rest of the way. The best thing she could think to do was to put as much distance between herself and Antonio as was possible.

What she did not realize was she had finally crossed the town limits of Haleton and was within the borders of Decaturville. The property Ivy now trod on belonged to the mayor of Decaturville, himself, Thomas Thistle. The tide was changing for Ivy and God had heard her plea. Thomas was a client of her father's and the owner of Duchess, the horse Ivy loved most. Fate had an odd way of working things out, and while Duchess never belonged to Ivy, it seemed there was a reason the two held such a tight bond. It could have been that Duchess knew the strength of the heart in Ivy or maybe the horse simply had a good judge of character. Either way, Ivanka Jessup exited the woods to find herself at the edge of the furthest pasture on Mayor Thistle's property. The mayor kept cattle out in those fields, and Ivanka peered around curiously as she slid her body between the barbed wire and fence posts. The poncho got caught on the wire and pulled her back so she lost her balance. Ivy screamed in pain as the hooks met with her skin and tore into her back. Fresh blood arose in beads as she pushed herself back up to a stand.

"It just never fucking ends!" she muttered as she began to tear up again. She tore the poncho from the fence and pulled it back over her head. It was now holed up and torn so much that it exposed her skin beneath in various places. Ivy looked back over the pasture and noticed a slight hill, where the sun peeked overhead. There, on top of it, was a huge house, and Ivy nearly flew towards it as she realized there were cars in the front. She ran and ran until, finally, she neared the next fence and barbed wire. This time, she was not in the least bit worried about the fencing tearing into her skin again. All she wanted was to get to that house. She slid between the wires and ran as fast as she could, towards the porch. She skipped up the steps, with tears welling in her eyes, and began to furiously beat on the door.

"Help! Help, please! Someone open the door, please! Please!" she wailed. For several minutes, nobody came to the door and Ivy slid to the ground, pulling her knees up to her chest as she leaned her back against the door, crying her eyes out. "Please, please, someone, please help me," she whispered between sobs.

"What is going o" Jane Thistle opened the door and looked down at the mess of a girl sitting on her porch. Her eyes widened and she finished her sentence, "Oh? Oh, my God. Are you okay? What happened to you?" Jane leaned down and looked Ivy over with concern and shock. It took Jane no time to realize that Ivy was completely naked, save for the tattered poncho with bloodstains.

Ivy looked up at her with red-rimmed eyes and began to sob even harder. "Oh, please let me have a phone to call my mother. Please?" she said to Jane. At this point, Ivy's mind was so fogged, she could not make out or identify who it was she was speaking to, but as the sunlight hit Jane Thistle's hair, it radiated around her, forming a halo of light. It reminded Ivy of a guardian angel and that was exactly what Jane decided to be.

"Oh, you poor girl. Come inside, and let's get you cleaned up then I will help you with a phone," she stated as she helped Ivy to her feet.

Ivy limped as Jane wrapped her arm around her and draped the other over her own shoulder. She helped Ivy over the threshold and immediately brought her to the den, where the fireplace was burning warmly. With ease, she placed Ivy in a recliner and placed a quilt over her body. The first thought on Jane's mind was to get the girl calm and then call the police. It was evident she had endured a sexual attack and brutalizing beating. "Just hush and rest there now, for a minute. I will bring you some tea and an icepack for your head, okay? Don't worry, you're safe now. You're safe, I promise," Jane reassured her.

Ivy shook her head and looked back at her with fear in her eyes. "No, no, please don't leave me. Please?" she cried out.

"I promise you will be safe. I have an alarm system here and four Rottweilers in a kennel, in the room next door. Plus, a twelve gauge rifle I know how to use. You are safe, honey. Just sit here for a minute, okay?" Jane stated. Ivy gave a sudden nod of agreement and leaned her head back against the recliner. She never drank the tea, because, by the time Jane brought it back to her, she had fallen asleep.

18

Proof Positive

A
ntonio wailed and screamed in fury as he tore through the house looking for Rosalia and Ivanka. Rosie would come back home he knew, as she had run out of the house in fear of him many times before. He never went after her because his worry of her getting far was slim to none. There were no other family members who could take Rosalia in, and because of that, Antonio counted on her coming back home every time she ran away. He peered at the clock and realized he needed to get to work and find Luis to help him find Ivy before his meeting with Jon Littleton came around.

"Just my pinche suerte!" Antonio roared. He slammed the door violently and stomped across the yard to his truck. The dirt picked up in a huge dust cloud as he sped down the driveway and pulled out onto the road. What was normally a twenty-minute drive, took him ten minutes and he pulled up to park at his job cursing agitatedly as he walked towards the entrance.

On the hill, just a few feet away, Aaron, Margie, and Wendy waited for Antonio to pull in. As soon as he did,

Margie nodded to Wendy and pushed Aaron's arm. "Let's go," she said.

Aaron eased the door open and stepped out, letting Margie slip from the truck after him.

Wendy went around to the back and pulled Lady to hop off the tailgate. "Come on, sweet Lady, let's go do some hunting, girl," she said sweetly. Lady snorted, and once again, Wendy held out a strip of the shirt for the dog to smell. Lady gave a light bark and signaled she had gotten enough scent to recognize Ivy. Wendy grinned. "Atta girl, let's go, guys," she said as Lady put her nose to the ground and began sniffing towards the parking lot. They crossed the road, and still, Lady kept leading them through the rows of cars towards one particular vehicle—Antonio Rodriguez's Ford Ranger.

The closer they got to the truck, the more Margie's heart began to flutter in worry and fear. Finally, Lady came to the vehicle and stood up on her hind legs peering inside the truck bed. She was on the side the rope was on, and as she sniffed, she turned back to Wendy and gave a light bark.

Wendy widened her eyes and looked down in the bed. "What you got there, Lady?" she asked. Lady gave another bark and snorted just as she had when she had first smelled Ivanka's shirt. "Do you see what she has sniffed out, Margie?" Wendy pointed, pulling the dog back from the truck bed.

Margie shook her head as her eyes fell upon the rope Jesse had explained was a hog tie, and Aaron looked down at the ground in disbelief.

"That's the rope. The rope you saw yesterday, Aaron?" she asked, turning back to look at him. "Damn it, that's it!" she exclaimed. Margie suddenly had the urge to waltz into the factory and beat Antonio Rodriguez's skull in with whatever blunt object she could find first. "I'll kill that mother fucker! I'll kill him!" she exclaimed.

Aaron immediately snapped out of his prior silence and

stepped forward to wrap his arms around Margie. "No, no. Don't go getting ahead of yourself, Margaret. We need to contact Kelvin and the police department. We need to get them to come out here with the bloodhounds or K9s and verify this. We can't do anything without them. It's vigilante justice. Listen, hush and listen, Margie," Aaron said.

Wendy nodded towards the direction of her truck and began walking back across the parking lot.

"Come on, let's go. We need to let people know about this as soon as possible. Margie, we would be wasting time going in there after Antonio on our own. Let the law do their job. Let's go find the guys and get down to the PD as Aaron suggested," she said.

Margie decided to use her better judgment and turned around, following after Wendy.

"You are both right, but I just..." She trailed her words and shook her head as tears welled in her eyes. Aaron had been right and Jesse had dismissed it as being a hog tie. It was a tie all right but not used for any hog. It had been used for their daughter! How could he call it a hog tie? There were so many things that went through Margie's head in a moment's notice that she did not know what to truly think. The worst fear she had was that the blood meant Ivanka was dead and there would be no finding her daughter alive. No hope for hearing her laughter or seeing her smile. No wedding and no grandchildren for her and Jesse to enjoy.

Aaron could sense it and he, too, was thinking that Ivy might not be found in the condition he had last seen her. The moment Aaron Kyle Kilpatrick had set eyes on Ivanka Jessup, he had been enamored of her, but in his attempt at being gentlemanly, he had lost the opportunity to tell her. The lyrics to a particular song entered his head, and he felt like crying.

"Life's a dance, you learn as you go..." It was a country song that had been really popular in the early nineties, by John

Michael Montgomery. The part that stuck out most in his mind was, *"When I was fourteen, I was falling fast for a blue-eyed girl in my homeroom class. Trying to find the courage to ask her out was like trying to get oil from a waterspout. What she would have said, I can't say. I never did ask before she moved away, but I learned something from my blue-eyed girl. Sink or swim, you've gotta give it a whirl."* Aaron sighed. If they found Ivy alive, the first thing he was going to do was kiss her the way a woman deserved to be kissed—fierce, possessive, protective, and endearing. Margie had wanted to kill Antonio, but if things went the way Aaron prayed they would, he was going to be the one to skin him alive. Love at first sight was so cliché`, but somehow, Aaron Kilpatrick had found himself a victim, and the possessor of his heart would be avenged. Somehow, someway, Aaron was hell-bent on it.

Antonio strode into the factory and went straight for Luis's station. "Oye, vato. I got some really bad fucking news," he began. "La puta got away. I don't know what time or when but she is fucking gone," he whispered.

Luis looked back at him and began shaking his head. "Are you serious, Tonio? I told ju I don't want anything more to do with this shit. I told ju that ju were in serious shit. Ju didn't listen. Chingada madre. How ju didn't know something would happen? Ju better take that fucking money of jurs and go talk to El Jefe. As for me, I fucking quit. Ju can handle this shit jurself," Luis said angrily.

Antonio narrowed his eyes and a pissed off expression crossed his face. "What the fuck ju saying, Luis? Ju know ju fucking helped get the bitch. Ju are just as much to blame as me, hijo de puta," he insulted.

Luis looked back at him and turned to walk away. "No, I

didn't do this stupid shit, ju did. I did grab her and ju know what? I'm going to tell the policia exactly what the fuck I did," he murmured, walking towards the exit.

Antonio stood wide-eyed with his mouth agape. He was now officially up shit creek without a paddle. The police were just one aspect to his problems. Jon Littleton and the cartel agreement was another. Antonio had no idea what he was going to do, but stopping Luis seemed to be the best solution, and all he could think of was murder.

Luis exited the factory and jogged over to his car. He knew that Antonio was a loose cannon and he had very little time to get things together. After confessing to his wife about his involvement in Ivanka's kidnapping, she had convinced him to go make a plea bargain with the police, in exchange for helping them find Ivy Jessup. Luis knew he faced jail time, but it was a price he was willing to pay in order to get his conscience clear and sever the tie with Antonio. He peeled out of the parking lot just as Antonio run out the building and started towards his truck. Time was of the essence but the good news was Ivanka was still alive, from what Antonio had confessed, and if Ivy got the help she needed, she would turn Luis in, anyway. The best plan was to get things squared away before the cops came looking for them both. Luis had more plans than just that, though. Luis knew enough about the entire drug setup in Decaturville and Haleton; his plan was to become a police asset and hope, maybe, just maybe, he could get off with that.

Ivy shuddered in her sleep and awoke abruptly when she felt hands on her shoulder. Her immediate response was to jump in her seat, and Jane stepped back, lifting both her hands in unison.

"It's all right, honey. I am just trying to wake you to let you know I have called the police and they are on their way. I also decided to get you some sweatpants and a sweater. I have a pair of house slippers here, too. I thought about asking you if you would like to shower, but I think it is best if we wait for the police to talk to you before you do anything like that," she said.

Ivy looked back at her and lifted her palm to rub her head. "Where am I, and who are you?" she asked confusedly.

"My name is Jane Thistle, and you are on the outskirts of Decaturville, Texas. Pretty close to Haleton, actually," she said.

Ivy dropped her hand and placed it on the armrest. "Have you called my mother yet?" she asked.

"No, honey. I don't even know your name. Where are you from?" Jane asked.

"Oh, um, my name is Ivanka Jessup. I'm from here, err, I mean Decaturville," she replied.

"Jessup? Are you Jesse and Margaret's daughter?" Jane asked with wide eyes.

Ivy looked at her, confused. "Um, yes. Do you know my parents?" she asked.

"Well, yes. My husband and I do business with them regularly. Who did this to you, honey?" she asked.

"I think I would rather tell the police that so I don't have to tell the story repeatedly. I really don't want to go through the whole ordeal over and over," she said in a whisper.

"I can understand that. I am truly sorry, honey. Can you tell me anything?" Jane asked.

"I was kidnapped from my job and held hostage for several

days. He…" She trailed her words and glanced away. "He raped me and forced me to perform heinous sexual acts." Suddenly, Ivy remembered about Rosalia and looked back at Jane with concern. "There is a little girl in his house, his sister. She needs to be gotten out of there. He is a psychopath, and she is only fourteen-years-old. Someone needs to save that little girl," Ivy explained.

"Okay, well, we will tell the police about that as soon as they get here. See if you can remember where you were held, if you know, that is," Jane said.

Ivy looked downward in realization that she had not gotten the address and had no idea what road the house was on.

"I can't remember that. Oh, no, what if he hurts that little girl?" she asked.

"Honey, we will find a way to get her out of there. Try not to worry anymore and just relax until the police get here. You have been through a very emotionally traumatizing experience. Go in the bathroom and change your clothes. Put that poncho in a plastic bag and tie it. We need to give that to the police for evidence, okay?" Jane asked.

"Yes, you are right. Thank you so much, Ms. Thistle. I really appreciate everything you have done for me. You are an angel," Ivy said. She leaned forward, and Jane placed the clothes in her palm.

"Right in there you go. I am sure the police will be here very soon," Jane said.

Ivy entered the bathroom quickly and shut the door. The urge to step under a steaming stream of water was really a hard temptation to fight, but Ivy knew the rape kit would need her to be as soiled as she had come in, for hardcore evidence in the case. She wanted to see Antonio fry under the Texas death penalty. As the old saying goes, the mirror tells no lies, and when Ivy looked at herself in the reflecting glass, she cringed in horror.

"Oh, my God," she muttered. It was a horrible display of blues and purples with angry red scratches all across her face. In truth, she looked like death warmed over, and it occurred to her why Jane had not recognized her. There was nothing recognizable about her, in the least. The appearance of Frankenstein's monster was what Antonio had turned her into. She leaned down towards the sink and splashed water on her face. Looking the way she did, she feared what her parents would say. What Aaron would say. What everyone would say. Ivy finished dressing quickly and exited the bathroom, just as Jane told her the police had arrived while she was in the lavatory and were waiting on her in the den.

"Good morning, miss. I am Officer Jenna Mills and this is my partner, Officer Lawrence Gillies. Can we ask you a few questions?" The female officer approached with a tiny notebook and a pen.

Ivy sat down and nodded. "Yes, but like I was telling Ms. Thistle, there is a little girl in the house I escaped from. She's fourteen. I don't know anything else about her, except that her name is Rosalia. I think her last name may be Rodriguez, but I'm not sure," Ivy said quickly.

The officer wrote down the name and gave a nod. "Okay, we will definitely do what we can to try to help her, but we need to find out where you were and who did this. Start from the beginning and tell us all you can remember, okay?" Jenna explained.

Ivy nodded. "I was kidnapped from my job two, maybe three, nights ago. Someone grabbed me from behind when I was taking out the trash. I think it was someone named Luis Velasquez, but I'm not sure. The sound of voice was familiar, and he is the person who is usually with the man who kept me," she said.

"And who was the man who kept you?" Jenna asked her.

"His name is Antonio Rodriguez. He had been giving me problems and got me fired from my old job at Bud's Motorbike Bar, down in Decaturville," Ivy said.

"Mind telling us what happened with that?" Jenna asked.

"Well, he tried to grab me one night at the bar and I hosed him down with draft beer. My boss fired me, and the next day, Antonio tried to cut us off at the red light, downtown. There was a disagreement and a scuffle with my father's new employee, Aaron Kilpatrick. Officer Kelvin Matthews wrote the report, I think. He told us to go on about our business and to avoid Antonio from there on out. So, we did just that. I got hired at Faraway Diner, and I had been working there all of three days when I got kidnapped. I know Antonio had me, because he raped me and he was the one who put all these cuts and bruises on me," Ivy explained.

"And what about the little girl, Rosalia? Where did she come in with all of this?" Jenna inquired.

"She was kind to me. She made sure I got something to eat, the first day, and some water. I could tell she did not like what her brother was doing, and she told me he would hurt her, that he has hurt her in the past. She didn't tell me if it was sexual abuse or not, but from the way she acted, she seemed petrified of him."

Jenna took down all the information and let her go on, telling all the specifics of the rape and brutality Antonio had placed her through. After half an hour, Jenna decided it was time to bring Ivy in.

"All right, Ivanka. I am going to take you into protective custody and get you to the hospital. When we get there, you are going to have to go through a really agonizing process, but it is needed so we can collect the evidence for an arrest and trial. I'm really sorry this happened to you, Miss Jessup. I promise I am going to do everything I can to help you," Jenna assured her.

"Well, can I please contact my parents? I really want to let my mom know I am okay. I'm sure she is worried sick, by now, and I just cannot go on not talking to her. Please?" Ivy asked.

"All right, Miss Jessup. I will let you use my cellphone in my patrol car and you can give your mom a call, but we still need to get you down to the hospital so they can get you through the rape kit and we can get a warrant for this Rodriguez guy," Jenna said.

Ivy looked back at Jane and smiled. "Thank you, Ms. Thistle. You saved my life. I don't know how I will ever repay you for that. Thank you so much," she said as she stood up to follow the officers out the door.

Jane smiled and waved it off. "Don't you worry, honey. I just want to see you home safe and get this guy behind bars so he can't hurt another girl around here. You take care, and when you get settled, you tell your mama to call us and let us know you are safe. I would really be grateful if you did that," Jane said.

Ivy nodded and crossed the room to hug the woman tightly. She let her go, smiling slightly, and exited behind the police officers. They helped her into the back of the squad car, and Jenna handed Ivy a phone as she sat in the seat.

"Go ahead and give your folks a call, honey. Make it quick and tell them you will be at the San Antonio Medical Center. They won't be able to look you up by name, so tell them to give me a call back at that number and I will tell them the name you are listed under in the hospital, okay?" Jenna stated.

"Okay, thank you," Ivy said. She lifted her fingers to begin dialing her mother's cellphone and waited silently.

Margie, Aaron, and Wendy pulled up at the police department to find Jesse and William already waiting for them. Each stepped from the truck and walked towards the front door.

"Jesse," Margie started as she walked towards him. "I'm sorry about blaming you, but you heard..." She trailed off into silence as her tears overtook her. Jesse pulled his wife into his embrace and held here there for a long moment.

"Hush now, baby. Hush, let's go inside and see what we can get Kelvin to do."

Just as the five of them were about to walk inside, Luis Velasquez pulled up and hurried through the entrance.

Jesse looked back at Aaron, confused, and nodded. "Let's get inside."

Willy and Wendy headed in first, and Aaron followed after. Jesse held Margie's hand as he walked her back into the police department. They entered, to hearing Luis's frantic voice trying to get someone to listen.

"Ju need to listen to me now! The missing girl is alive. I am telling ju. I have a lot of information to give. Ju just need to listen!" he said.

Kelvin looked past Luis and noticed the rest of the group standing there. It seemed everyone in the department was there to discuss Ivanka Jessup.

"Now, just wait a minute, all right? Let me talk to these people first, okay?" Kelvin said, brushing Luis to the side, "What are you all doing here?" He directed the question more at Jesse and Margie than anyone else, but it was Wendy who piped up first.

"Kelvin, you have used our certified bloodhounds, on a number of occasions, in searching for suspects around here. Well, I am telling you that Antonio Rodriguez has had Ivanka in the back of his pickup truck. Before you go reprimanding me for snooping, I was hired by the Jessups, whether paid or not, to provide a legal service. Lady sniffed out Ivy's scent on a rope that is covered in blood in the back of Antonio's truck down at the Fillmore Plant," Wendy explained.

"Ju see, I have to tell ju some things!" Luis exclaimed.

"Okay, I hear what you are saying, Wendy. Listen, you all sit down and let me get Luis's statement, okay? I'll be right back to talk to you," Kelvin said. He knew that a girl had been called in, about thirty minutes prior to the arrival of everyone else. What he did not know was if the girl was Ivanka, and his officers had just gone out to the Thistle home to pick her up. There was not much of a description to go off of, but Kelvin was hoping it was Ivy. He decided not to give the Jessups or anyone else the head's up just yet, in case it wound up being someone else.

"Fine, we will sit right here and shut up," Jesse said, taking a seat across from the desk.

Kelvin frowned and waved Luis to a back office. "Come on, Luis. Let's go have a chat, shall we?" he said, walking towards the back room. The rest of the crew just watched in silence, taking their seats impatiently as Luis followed Kelvin into the office. The door creaked to a close and time seemed to stop in its tracks.

19

'Fess Up

"**A**ll right, Luis, 'fess up," Kelvin said, taking a seat and pointing to the one across from him.

"Before I tell ju anything, I want to ask about becoming a police asset or whatever ju call them. A tip man or how you call it? A narc?" he asked.

"You want to be a narc for us. This must be some hell of a story," Kelvin said.

"Well, yes. I have been doing some bad shit around here, Officer Matthews. Got myself into a lot of shit I did not need to be into. I have a wife and a little three-year-old daughter. I don't want to make their lives hard and the information I can tell ju is dangerous for me but is most dangerous for my wife and child. Ju understand?" Luis said.

Kelvin nodded. "Yeah, I am following you, Luis. I'm interested in what you have to say. Go on. I will take into consideration your offer to be an informant," Kelvin said.

Luis started going into detail about Jon Littleton, the drugs he was pushing, his cartel connections and what Antonio had planned with Ivy. The conversation lasted a while, and Kelvin listened intently as every detail of the awful ordeal was explained.

Antonio pulled up at Jon's junkyard, nervous as a deer in headlights. He didn't know what to tell Jon or how to explain his fuck up, and the words for it were coming up blank every second. Much to his relief, Jon was not in the office the moment he pulled up and it gave him a few minutes to consider everything he needed to tell the man. The thought of booking had occurred to him, but Rosie still wandered somewhere and she needed him. In some twisted way, Antonio had still maintained he had a responsibility to his little sister. He snorted and wiped his nose on his sleeve, tapping the steering wheel nervously as he waited. Time seemed to creep by, and finally, Tonio decided to head back to the house. Maybe he would get lucky, if he checked the land, and Ivy would show up somewhere. He sped through town, nervous as hell, but the quick driving brought him to the house in ten minutes. Sure enough, Rosalia had come back and was busying herself preparing some lunch when Antonio came in.

"Hermano, I am sorry. You scared me really bad, earlier. I had to get some air," Rosie said.

Antonio glanced over at her and shook his head. "I'm sorry, Rosalia. I know ju didn't do anything to help la puta. Ju had every chance to do so the whole day she stayed with ju and ju didn't. I have to find her or I am going to go away for a long, long time. Bad men will come looking for me, Rosalia," he said.

Rosie gave a sigh, but she knew it was only a matter of time before Antonio was picked up for his crimes. This last moment with her brother, she chose to use as a chance to point him towards redemption.

"Hermano, you should pray to God and ask him to forgive you. Ask for him to help you and make it where you will not have to face him as a bigger judge for your sins," Rosie said sadly.

Antonio sighed and slid down to his knees, sobbing. He was screwed; there was no getting past it and Rosie's words were just the icing on his shit cake.

Luis finished telling the story, and Kelvin finally emerged from the office, leaving him to sit.

The phone rang in Margie's pocket and she pulled it out to glance over the caller ID. *Unknown Number Decaturville Texas,* the screen read. "Hello, Margie Jessup speaking," she said as she answered.

"Mama?" Ivy whispered hoarsely. "Mama, it's me. It's Ivy," she cried over the speaker. Margie's eyes filled with tears and she jumped from her seat. At that same moment, Officer Mills radioed in to let Kelvin know what had happened at the Thistle place.

"This is Officer Jenna Mills, Kelvin, we got Ivanka Jessup. We will be taking her to San Antonio for the rape kit," she said.

Kelvin cut the transmission down so nobody else would hear, but Margie was too ecstatic in her reply for anyone to know what was being said.

"Ivanka? Oh, my God, Ivanka!" Margie screamed. "Where are you? We will come get you, right now! Who took you? Mama loves you so much!" Each sentence was said so quickly, it was hard to decipher where one began and the other ended.

Ivy smiled on the other end and whispered into the phone, "Mama, the police have me. They are taking me to San

Antonio Medical Center. The officer whose phone I called you from said you can call her back at this number and she will give you the name to find me under, there," Ivy explained between jagged breaths.

"But the number didn't show up, Ivy," Margie said in a worrisome tone.

"It's okay, Mama. She said she would talk to you. Just talk to her. I need to go now. I love you. Please be ready to get me from San Antonio," she whispered.

Aaron listened closely during the entire exchange and was able to hear Ivy's voice. A sudden chill came over him and he realized all he wanted was to get to that hospital and see Ivy, alive and well. The rest of the group all gave loud claps and exclamations of joy. Somehow, Ivanka had made it through it and was alive.

"Well, I guess you all now know Ivanka is alive," Kelvin said. "Luis, in there, just gave a full confession, and he is going to help us get Antonio," he finished.

"Oh, really? Why is that?" Jesse asked, confused.

"I guess because Antonio went off the deep-end and Luis feels like he needs to cut ties with the looney-tune. You all head on up to San Antone, now, and quit worrying about the police work. With the tip the Hearles have given us here, I'll go looking in Antonio's truck for the rope and collect it as evidence. For now, we have enough to get a warrant and I need to call the judge to get it written up. Apparently, from what my officers out at the Thistle place discovered, Antonio had a teenage girl up there and she needs to be gotten out before he hurts somebody," Kelvin finished. They all nodded and filed out. Everyone got into his or her vehicles, and Aaron decided to cross the street to his car.

"I'm going to drive up there myself, Mr. and Mrs. Jessup. I will meet you there, okay?" he said.

Margie and Jesse got into the truck and immediately

headed towards the interstate. The convoy to pick up Ivanka had begun and the family was united in support for her. The police had this investigation in the bag, and Margie finally had the peace she needed to just let them do their jobs.

Kelvin pulled up at the Rodriguez place, an hour later, and stepped out. There were three other patrol cars behind him as he walked towards the door. He pounded on it with force. "Antonio, open up and come on out here," Kelvin said.

The door creaked open, but the face he saw was of a very pretty Hispanic girl with wavy black hair and wide brown eyes.

"Are you Rosalia?" Kelvin asked.

Rosie nodded and stepped outside. "Yes, I am Rosalia. My brother is inside, drunk, and I think he is high, too. He keeps talking about bad men coming for him and demons. I'm scared," she said.

Kelvin pointed towards the police cars and urged her down to them. "Go on down there and get in one of the cars. They will help you and we'll get you out of here, okay?" Kelvin instructed.

Rosie ran out of the house and directly for the cop cars.

Kelvin walked inside and called out for Tonio. In seconds, he noticed Antonio lying on the ground with a bottle of tequila in hand.

"Ju are here to arrest me for what I did to la puta. That pinche puta, she ruined my life. I am telling ju, she ruined it. Ay, what am I going to do?" he screamed.

Kelvin pulled his gun out and ordered Antonio to stand up. "Antonio Rodriguez, stand up and face the wall. Put your hands behind your head and do not move. You are under arrest for the kidnapping and assault of Ivanka Jessup." He stepped towards him as Antonio followed his instructions. "You have the right to remain silent, and you have the right to an attorney." He explained his entire Miranda Rights and began cuffing him. Antonio sobbed and was led out the front door in shame. Kelvin placed him in the back of the patrol car and drove him down to the jail. It was the end of the line for Antonio Rodriguez.

20

Family Reunion

Ivanka spent hours going through the grueling process of a rape kit, and when her parents were finally able to collect her to go home, she was shocked to see Aaron's handsome face peeking in the hospital room behind them.

"Oh, no! Don't look at me. I look hideous!" she exclaimed. In the midst of everything that had happened to her, Ivy did not want Aaron to see her looking like such a wreck.

Aaron shook his head and pushed past Margie and Jesse. "Do you mind if I have a minute alone with Ivy, please?" he asked.

Jesse looked upset by the question and immediately shook his head. "No, I don't think so," Jesse said.

Margie squeezed his hand and pulled him towards the door. "No, come on, honey. I need some coffee. Let's go get some, okay?" She urged him out of the room. Jesse looked upset by it but agreed and followed her outside.

Aaron walked to the side of Ivy's bed and slid his index finger beneath her chin. "Ivy, look at me, honey," he said sweetly.

Ivy looked up at him and teared up.

"You are beautiful, Ivanka Jessup. I knew it the moment I laid eyes on you. I think I dreamed you into existence," he said, lowering his lips to press a gentle feather light kiss against hers.

Ivy inhaled gently and pressed her lips back against his. It was as if they fit perfectly together and this was always meant to happen. Aaron pulled her close into his arms and held her there as he deepened the kiss and explored her mouth. His tongue slid gently over hers and he moved his lips slowly, leisurely, almost in tease.

Ivy broke away and looked down, embarrassed by her reaction.

"Oh, I'm...I feel..." She trailed her words and stared at the floor.

Aaron lifted her chin to peer into her eyes again and shook his head. "No, sweet Ivy. Let me be the one to heal your pain. Let me love you. I have, ever since the first day I laid eyes on you. Nobody will ever hurt you again, I promise. Just give me the chance," he said.

Ivy's heart skipped a beat in that moment, and she realized it was the hope that Aaron cared about her that had kept her going. It was the few moments they had spent together. The horseback riding and the way he made her laugh in the moments she should have been crying. Moments just like the one they were in. She pulled him back towards her and kissed him fervently. All she could have ever wanted existed in one man, Aaron Kilpatrick. She smiled as she released him, just as her parents walked back in.

The discharge nurse came back with the release forms for Ivy to sign so she could home and the family exited the hospital, relieved to be complete again.

Margie knew that whatever had happened between Aaron and Ivy, in those brief moments, would set the pace for their relationship, and she hoped that all would go just as she had thought it would all along.

Six Months Later

Aaron chased Ivy around his couch, and she giggled with wild glee as she raced towards their back bedroom. Ever since Ivy had gotten home, she had been spending all of her time in Aaron's barn apartment. As a gift, the Thistles had signed the paperwork and ownership of Duchess to Ivy and she preferred spending her time close to the two things she loved most, Aaron and Duchess. Aaron pounced Ivy as she fell onto the bed and pinned her down as he began to lay kisses against her throat. "Stop, baby!"

She squirmed in delight as he continued to caress her throat. His left hand slid down to the button on her pants and popped it open with an easy and quick snap. Ivy continued to giggle as Aaron pushed up her shirt and laid his lips against her bare stomach. Slowly, he shimmied her pants off and placed a sweet kiss against the hem of her panties. Ivanka drew in a soft breath and looked down at him in surprise. Aaron caught her gaze and grinned as he slid his hands between the cotton and her skin. Gently, he placed the tip of his index finger atop her clitoris and began to rub it in circular motions. Ivy sucked in a breath and began to breath in quick, shallow breaths.

He continued his torture on her, by lowering his mouth over her stomach and beginning to slide his finger further down her already wet slit. With his free hand, he began to pull her underwear downward and eased them from her body. His mouth quickly found the center of her sweet cunt and began to suckle on it as his finger slid deep inside her tight, wet hole. With easy motions, Aaron continued to please her, gently pulling his finger in and out of the soft velvety folds of her heated core. Ivy groaned in delight and pulled him from his feasting, only to draw him immediately down to her lips.

Her free hand slid down to grab the bulge in his pants and she breathed against his mouth, eager for more. "Please, baby. Fuck me like I'm yours," she whimpered. That was all Aaron needed to convince him and he pulled his thick cock free of his pants without any hesitation. Gently, he eased himself down to plunge into the grip of her sweet pussy. With a thrust of his hips, he felt her open up over him and moaned deeply as she pulled him closer to her body. Aaron began to quicken his pace as Ivy lifted her legs to wrap about his waist and clawed her nails into his shoulders.

"You never need to ask me twice, baby," he murmured gently against her lips. His hand slid through her platinum locks and he cradled her cheek against his palm. "You never cease to amaze me, Ivy. God, you are so beautiful," he said in a sweet tone.

Ivy grinned and lifted her pelvis to meet with his next thrust. Each movement he made brought her closer and closer to the peak of ecstasy, and Aaron could see it in her eyes. It increased his desire to please her even more, and he began to furiously pump himself in and out of her sweet, hot folds. He shuddered as he drew closer to climax and struggled to keep himself from exploding from the sheer intensity of their lovemaking. She pulled him closer and moaned hard into his mouth as her muscles began to contract in succession about his throbbing prick. Ivy leaned her head backward and screamed, "Mmm, baby, you stretch me so well, and I can't help but..." Ivy's words were cut off by Aaron closing his mouth over hers and shuddering as he ejaculated. He pulled back, just as the last shiver ran down his spine.

"Ivanka Jessup, will you marry me?" he asked as he stared deep into her eyes.

Ivy smiled and gave a nod. "Only if you promise to love me like this, every single night," she teased but quickly became serious. "Of course, Aaron Kilpatrick. I could not want anything more than to be your wife." Aaron pulled her close and cradled her. There they rested, falling into a deep sleep with dreams of their future dancing in both of their heads.

Epilogue

A ntonio Rodriguez was sentenced to the death penalty after a four-month trial that was helped by the testimonies of Luis Velasquez, Wendy Hearle, and Rosalia Rodriguez, along with Ivanka's own account of the kidnapping. With the help of Luis, Jon Littleton's entire junkyard front was taken down and he was charged with sex ring trafficking, drug trafficking, and prostitution. Luis helped bring down the biggest supplier of crime in the cities of Haleton and Decaturville. Antonio was sent to the Texas Department of Corrections.

Ivanka Jessup gave birth to a beautiful baby boy that same month. She and Aaron had been married for three months, when their son, Brenton Kyle Kilpatrick was born. They chose to name him in honor of Ivy's brother and Aaron's middle name, which was his grandfather's middle name. Margie and Jesse were ecstatic to be grandparents, and the Jessup Farm seemed to have life flourishing upon their land once again.

Sai Marie Johnson

Sai Marie is an author, creative writer, and concept creator. She resides in the Great Pacific Northwest where she enjoys the flora, fauna, action and adventure that bred the Pioneer Spirit. With a heart for advocacy, animals, the environment, and great imagination, she is sure to capture your attention with something for everyone.

Visit her website here:
http://www.saimariejohnson.wordpress.com

Visit her blog here:
http://www.saimariejohnson.blogspot.com

Don't miss these exciting titles by Sai Marie and Blushing Books!

<u>Simply Scarlet</u>
<u>The Softer Side of Texas</u>
Embracing His Empire

Blushing Books

Blushing Books is the oldest eBook publisher on the web. We've been running websites that publish steamy romance and erotica since 1999, and we have been selling eBooks since 2003. We have free and promotional offerings that change weekly, so please do visit us at http://www.blushingbooks.com/free.

Blushing Books Newsletter

Please join the Blushing Books newsletter
to receive updates & special promotional offers.
You can also join by using your mobile phone:
Just text **BLUSHING** to 22828.

Every month, one new sign up via text messaging will receive
a $25.00 Amazon gift card, so sign up today!